Joyce,
I hope you enjoy!
Thank you for your support.
WMason Dunn

More than Sisters

Written by W. Mason Dunn

Copyright 2015 W. Mason Dunn

Dedicated
To
Henry and Viola Johnson

Acknowledgements

I would first like to acknowledge the one who planted the seed and brought it to completion. All praise, honor and glory to my Lord and Savior, Jesus Christ.

My husband, Donald, who is still the world's finest Marine.

I would like to thank my children-Ashley and Michael. I am so grateful that God chose me to serve as your mother.

I am thankful to have been born the sister of Judi Ann Mason, who believed in me when I did not believe in myself. I miss you so much, but we will meet again.

To my literary manager Phyllis Larrymore-Kelly, thank you for your labor of love.

Joseph Burgess, thank you for your candid thoughts and your professional perspective.

My editor and friend, Ann Marie Bryan and Victorious by Design, thank you for everything. It has been a blessing to work with you.

Global Multi Media Enterprises, your supernatural creativity is from out of this world. Thank you for designing the cover.

To my proofreaders, Ashley Dunn, Drew Holcombe and Dianna Whitmore, thank you for your sacrifice.

TABLE OF CONTENTS

CHAPTER 1

Dani was nine years old when she was kidnapped from the front porch of her grandmother's house. Her captors knew exactly how to entice her.

Chocolate.

Most kids loved chocolate, and Dani was no exception.

She lived in an all-black neighborhood in Shreveport, Louisiana. An assortment of small red, gray, maple and white brick homes lined both sides of Madison Avenue. No two houses were alike. However, they had one thing in common … the security that comes from being among your own kind in the racist south. One could exist for days and never see a white person outside of television. The community contained schools, shops, churches, and even government services. Racial tensions were peaking in Shreveport in 1972. The Police Service Commissioner had blocked local civil rights movements and folks were trying to make it safely from one day to the next.

Yet within the safety of her own neighborhood, Dani was allowed to be in only one or two places-her house or her Grandmother's house, which was two houses down.

Her best friend was Mrs. Beasley, whose head was made of vinyl. A pair of square black plastic glasses framed her face. She was a blonde-haired baby doll with a soft blue and white polka dot body. They sat in our imaginary kitchen on the front porch of grandmother's small, redbrick home. Sitting in the white metal tulip chair, Dani changed Mrs. Beasley into her new red dress.

The sound of a car slowing down in front of the house pulled Dani away from the land of make-believe. A two-door, white Chevy Impala pulled up and parked at the front curb and a woman got out.

The caramel-colored young woman walked toward Dani. She wore a tie-dyed tunic and white polyester bellbottoms. She smiled at Dani the way a relative would smile when seeing a long-lost loved one.

The woman knelt down next to Dani and said, "I have something for you in my car." The woman took Dani and Mrs. Beasley by the hand and walked toward the parked car.

"Do you see that candy?" asked the woman, pointing to the back seat. Dani could see the bag of Hershey chocolates waiting for her.

"Yes."

Dani jumped across the front seat toward the candy. The sweat from her legs squeaked against the vinyl seats as she made her way to the bag. Mommee would never allow her to eat candy before lunch. However, Mommee was at work and would never find out.

Before she could put the first piece of chocolate in her mouth, they were speeding down the street.

Out of the rear window, Dani could see Grandmother's house moving farther and farther away. She never saw Mommee or Grandmother again.

CHAPTER 2

Dani

Three months earlier

Dani knew she was cool the day her big sister, Gayle, invited her to walk to the corner store. Gayle plunked herself down on the edge of the bed and said, "Dani, want to go with me?"

Gayle was 17-years-old, and Dani stood in awe of everything about her. Gayle was smart, curvaceous and brave enough to say exactly what was on her mind. It seemed she was forever in trouble for the words that rolled out of her mouth.

She studied Gayle and waited for the day that her nine-year-old boyish body mirrored that of her sister's.

"Really, you want me to go with you?"

"Sure, go ask Gertrude."

Gayle called Mommee by her first name, Gertrude; a privilege Dani assumed would be hers upon becoming a teenager.

Gertrude was peeling potatoes in the kitchen. She wore a yellow, flowered cotton housedress covered by a white cotton apron and she gazed out of the kitchen window.

"Mommee, can I go to the store with Gayle? I promise to stay right next to her."

"No, you know you can't go with her. You are not going anywhere with that fast-tail girl. And tell her she had better hurry up and get her lazy butt back here so I can finish dinner before your daddy gets home."

Dani turned to find Gayle standing in the kitchen doorway and waited for the explosion that was certain to follow. Gayle's eyes shouted words at Gertrude that Dani would not be allowed to repeat. Then Gayle looked at her little sister, winked, smiled and headed for the front door.

Gertrude turned back to the window and continued peeling the potatoes.

Dani trailed close behind Gayle, ready to grab the door before it was sure to slam. She sat on the small concrete front porch and waited for her sister's return.

CHAPTER 3

Olivia

Olivia was a confident woman.
Her voice was confident.
Her walk was confident.
Her attitude was confident.
Everything about Olivia was confident.

It had been a crazy day. After having to do her job and the job of two other people who had called in sick at the last minute, Olivia could not wait to get home. She was tired and all she wanted to do was unwind on the couch and play with her little girl, Tasha.

Olivia parked the car in the carport of the small three-bedroom home. She unlocked the side door, entered the dining room, and listened as her husband finished a telephone call.

"Yes, sir. Thank you," Leonard said.

He hung up the phone.

"Who was that?" she asked.

"Oh, I didn't hear you come in. That was the principal at Butler Elementary School. I won't be teaching at Butler Elementary next year."

"I'm sorry baby. Maybe you'll find something tomorrow." She wanted to take him into her arms and tell him everything would be all right. However lately, being close to each other seemed to be the last thing that was on their minds.

Instead, she walked passed him and opened the oven door. "Oh, I forgot to put in the leftovers. I am sorry. I'll do it now," he said.

"Where's Tasha?"

"She's in her room. She might be asleep."

"Asleep? Remember I asked you to keep her up so she wouldn't give me trouble when it is time for her to go to bed tonight?"

Olivia watched as Leonard turned the knob to heat the oven.

"Well did she at least do her homework?"

"I don't think she had any."

"Did you check her bag? Forget it. I'll do it myself."

There was a time when Leonard was the love of her life. They met in Arizona where she was singing in a nightclub. He came into the club with a group of other teachers. When she finished singing, he offered to buy her a drink and they talked all night. It was love at first sight and they were married within two years.

That was ten years ago.

Now their union was cold and detached.

Olivia left Arizona to help her family out when her mother got sick.

Leonard joined her shortly afterwards.

CHAPTER 4

Gayle

The next day, Gayle sat alone in her bedroom doing homework. Daddy left to pick Gertrude up from work and Dani would be home from school soon so she used some of the extra time alone to write in her diary.

"Gayle ..." Dani yelled as soon as she entered the house.

"I'm back here."

Dani rushed to the back of the house.

She did not bother putting her school things away.

"What's a stepmother?" asked Dani.

The question startled Gayle.

"A stepmother is a woman who marries your father after your mother leaves or dies. Why do you want to know what a stepmother is?"

"My friend Enid said that her mamma knew my mamma before she died and that Mommee was my stepmother."

Gayle looked at Dani and motioned for her to sit on the bed.

Dani said, "Mommee is our mamma and she's not dead, she's at work. Daddy went to go get her like he always does, right?"

Gayle took a deep breath.

"Gertrude is not our mother."

Her words faded as Dani stared in disbelief.

"Yes, she is ..." Dani said throwing her books on the bed. Her eyes dampened, her lips trembled and her nose sniveled.

Gayle reached for her little sister's hand and said, "I knew this day would come ..."

Gayle knelt down beside her bed and reached under the mattress. She pulled out an envelope.

"I wrote this so I could tell you all about Mama when you were ready. Would you like me to read it to you?"

Dani nodded.

"Are you sure?"

"Yes."

She pulled a few pages from the envelope and began reading.

> *Dear Dani,*
>
> *The tall, charcoal woman of grace gleamed with a soft voice that seldom, if ever, went above a soprano whisper.*
>
> *Mama was soft.*
>
> *Her voice was soft. Her walk was soft. Her every day attitude was soft. Rose was the softest mother God ever made.*
>
> *I suppose I could be accused of favor. Mama shone with God's favor and one could only dream of this type of mother. I think she was patterned after the mother of Jesus.*
>
> *She sang a lot, especially around the house, early in the morning with the birds.*
>
> *As she prepared hearty breakfasts for her family, she hummed "Amazing Grace" or "I can see so much what the Lord has done for me."*

Oh, how gentle – and soft - was that voice! Even when she "scolded" one of her children, she never screamed. She was never angry with any of her children. She simply stated her point as they strained to hear any note of anger. Anger was never in her voice – just frankness.

The skinny, but healthy, lady loved surprises. In the first grade, at odd times, she would pop in on my class with cookies and candy for all the kids. Needless to say, the class was almost as thrilled as I was.

God, I think now, how blessed we are to have had such a woman to call mama. She would always do little things that made the family smile.

She worked as a maid for a well–to–do white family, while keeping her home spotless, doing most of the work herself. All of it she did herself, once Olivia left home.

She scolded her children for flying off at the mouth, being "too grown," being lazy and letting friends take advantage of them.

She loved to brush my hair, dress me in pink and rock me to sleep in the old, creaky rocking chair while singing "Sweet Low Sweet Chariot."

She made good pancakes, biscuits and fried chicken.

Her mother's name was Lula, but all the grandchildren called her LuBill. Mama was very obedient to her mother.

She always seemed healthy, which is why it was a surprise when she had to go to the hospital. However, she took time out, months before, to prepare her children for a departure that would take her to Shumpert Hospital never to return to 5201 Rick Street.

It seemed that out of nowhere, Mama got quite strict on me. Instead of letting me play with my friends, as usual, I was made to stay inside to learn how to make up beds, boil chicken and change my one-year old sister's diapers – you.

I resented the change. Mama made me iron daddy's handkerchiefs. I had to hang out clothes on the clothesline. Frustrated because other seven-year-old girls were not doing it, I cried and begged mama to tell me why I had to do all that.

"Nobody is going to want to take care of you if you can't do these things."

"I don't care," I retorted.

"Gayle, just turn around and iron. What are you going to do if I'm not around to take care of you?"

That thought sent shock waves.

Mama not around?

Inconceivable.

Mama would always be around...

A few weeks later, Mama packed a suitcase and climbed into the Chevy with Daddy to go to the hospital.

Life was terribly lonely without her around the house. Daddy, who was usually full of bubbly fun, moped around the house, fumbling with you and me on his hands in a way completely foreign to him. Soon after, Olivia came home from Arizona to care for us. Mama was desperately missed.

I was not allowed to visit Mama in the hospital. I begged and begged but they kept telling me I was too young. I cried but Daddy said the hospital would not allow it.

Then even more desperate, I prayed to Jesus. The friend Mama sang to and talked with often. I cried to God for mercy. Days passed, then one second Sunday in the middle of summer on the way home from church, Daddy and I were driving alone. He asked me, "Gayle, would you like to see your mama?"

"Yes, sir!"

"Okay," he said, "Your mama wants to see you, too."

I was exuberant.

I began to sing with daddy right there in the car. My prayer had been answered.

The hospital was an awesome place. Yet it was a pleasant place to be because I would finally see Mama, our mama, our lovely beautiful mother whose cheeks glowed with love and tenderness always, whose eyes rejoiced in life, whose voice chimed with birds.

I could hardly wait.

She was on the second floor.

Quiet.

Still.

Our shoes clicked on the floor with fluttering impatience. Daddy stopped, pushed open a door and there she lay.

She wore none of the freshly ironed print dresses she wore at home. Her starched apron was not around her. She was lying flat on her back in a mousey white hospital gown amid mousey white sheets. Her flowing salt and pepper locks were uncurled and stretching in odd directions. How odd that was, because Mama always kept her hair neat and curled.

Eyes half-closed, Mama turned to see us walking toward her bed. She smiled faintly, slowing breaking into a widened grin. She tried to open her eyes wider but they kept folding down again.

Mama looked so tired, so different, so distant. Yet she glowed with recognition of me. Her feeble hand reached for me and she tugged me to her breast.

"Hi, mama..."

We spoke. Mama asked if I had been a good girl. She asked about school.

About you.

About other things... yet when she spoke of you, she spoke with concern unmatched by anything else.

"I want you to take care of Dani."

"Okay. When are you coming home, Mama?"

She did not answer. She just asked, "Has Dani been a good baby?"

"Yeah, Mama. When are you coming home?"

"Mama might not come home."

What? I did not know what to think then. Maybe I thought Mama was just trying to get me to do housework again.

She repeated, "Mama might not come home...but I want you to be a good girl and take care of your baby sister."

"Okay," I managed to utter, never so shocked in my life. I never knew anyone who deserved to live more than our mother did. She was kind to everyone, sharing, loving, and gentle.

"Mama is going to have to die, Gayle," she said quite frankly.

Death.

It meant I would not see our mother again in the flesh. Tears filled my eyes, but they only dropped in big chunks. She said many things but I was trying to imagine life without her. Mama told me not to cry, but I could not help it.

After a while, Mama's eyes opened wide and she tried to laugh, tried to make me laugh, make Daddy laugh.

And she did.

She took off her wedding ring and told me to keep it. She hugged me and told me with blessed assurance "I will see you soon, baby..."

We left the hospital when visiting hours were over. I left a different eight year old. I felt eighty-eight. Mama had never lied to me. How I wished Mama would have then.

However, it was true.

The following Saturday morning, Daddy came home from spending all night in the hospital. I ran outside. He was leaning against the car, arms folded. He told me Mama was dead.

You were then a tiny baby who would never know her voice. You would never remember her warm, loving arms around you, her soft angelic voice singing in your ears. She did promise one thing; she would see us in heaven. She will probably be a lead soprano soloist in the heavenly choir.

Gayle placed the letter on the bed, and held Dani in her arms.

They wept together.

"She loved you so much, Dani ..."

"But ... but how come I don't remember any of this. I thought Mommee was ..."

"You thought I was what?"

Gertrude stood at the bedroom door with her hands on her hips and her eyes wider than a deer caught in the headlights.

CHAPTER 5

Dani

Reverend Ferguson stood Goliath tall and his presence commanded respect from those around him. But he felt like he was losing ground as he reprimanded his daughter that evening.

"It wasn't your place to tell her anything!" he said.

"I did not tell her. She heard it at school. You had to know that she would eventually find out," Gayle said.

"Don't get smart with me ... I get to decide when and what she knows. You are not her mother."

"And neither is Gertrude!"

The yelling bounced off the thin walls of the master bedroom into the girls' room and through the pillow covering Dani's ears.

When she couldn't take any more of the arguing, Dani tried to intervene.

Reverend Ferguson turned to see Dani standing at the door.

"Dani, get back in your room."

For a few seconds it was a staring contest complete with blazing gaze lines. Reverend Ferguson collapsed into his recliner in the corner of the room. His chocolate-brown eyes sat evenly apart above his high cheekbones and alongside his broad nose. The patriarch looked at his youngest daughter and then held his head down.

The room was tense and silent.

After a moment, he said, "It's true, baby girl your mama is dead."

CHAPTER 6

Gayle

A solemn Gayle sat on the bed, her eyes swollen and her face powdered with dried tears. Dani lay on the bed next to her, holding on tightly to Mrs. Beasley.

"I remember being in second grade when Mama's stomach began to grow larger," said Gayle. "I didn't bother to ask why. But one day Mama sat me down. With no words minced, Mama said, 'Gayle, I want to tell you something.'"

"Ma'am?" I asked, always enjoying mama's few words.

"Have any of the children been saying anything to you about my stomach?"

"No ma'am," I replied, embarrassed, perhaps, because I had been wondering about the strange change in Mama's physique.

"Well, there's a baby in my stomach," Mama added, watching my eyes light up with joy and surprise.

"We're going to have a baby?"

"Yes."

"A boy or a girl?"

"Which one do you want?"

"A girl! Can I make up a name?"

"Mama was just as excited about the baby, as I was. She told me the approximate date when "she" would arrive and promised me that it would be my baby too. I thought for certain I had as much to do with the expected as mama and daddy did."

She looked intently at Dani and added, "No matter what happens after this, I will never regret telling you about mama."

CHAPTER 7

Olivia

"So you're still not talking to me?" Leonard said as he entered the bedroom that night. He began to unbutton his shirt and change into his pajamas.

Olivia turned away from the mirror where she had been brushing her hair but did not respond.

"You haven't said a word to me since you stormed out of the living room. Liv, I am sorry, but we just cannot afford to buy a new washer. The old one is working just fine."

"I'm sorry too, Leonard. But-"

"Let me finish. I will find a job that will help to dig us out of this hole. I take my role as Head of this Household seriously. I haven't given up and I don't want you to give up either."

Olivia turned to her husband. She realized she never loved him more than she did at that moment.

"I won't give up either, if you promise to let me know when you've had enough."

Leonard looked at her with questions in his eyes.

"What do you mean, if I've had enough?"

"We both know that you regret moving here from Arizona," said Olivia.

"Is that what you think? You think I regret leaving Arizona?"

"Yes, you gave up your job to come to Louisiana so I could take care of my mother and then you stayed so I could help Daddy take care of my sisters. And I-"

"Hold on. I loved your mother. So don't even open your mouth to say that I regret it."

Leonard flailed his hands in irritation, before sliding under the bed covers.

"Gayle and Dani are my sisters too. You have been through more than anybody should go through in a lifetime. But I do have regrets. I regret not being able to help more. But I promise I will find a job, and I will take care of this family."

Olivia took Leonard in her arms and kissed him.

Leonard returned the favor with a deep-seated and sensuous kiss, interrupted by the ringing of the phone.

Olivia gently pulled away.

Leonard smiled offhandedly.

"Hello," Olivia said into the phone.

"Olivia, could you come and get me?" said Gayle.

She could scarcely get the words out without crying.

"Gayle? What's wrong?"

"I ran away …I can't go back there. Please come and get me."

"Tell me where you are, and I'll be right there."

CHAPTER 8

Dani

The next morning, Gertrude entered the girls' bedroom.

Dani pried open her eyes.

"Come on get up, Dani. Gayle must be in the bathroom. You go in the bathroom when she gets out."

"Yes, ma'am."

Dani rose slowly from her bed. But as soon as Gertrude walked away, she laid back down for a little more uninterrupted sleep.

After a few minutes, Dani could hear the adults talking in the other room. The tone of their voices told her that something serious was going on.

She decided to investigate.

She saw her father and Gertrude at the kitchen table, each cradling a cup of coffee.

"Dani, go in the bathroom and brush your teeth. You need to get ready for school," Gertrude said.

"Where's Gayle?"

"Don't worry about Gayle?" replied Gertrude.

"But where is she?"

He reached into the kitchen drawer for a pack of Camel cigarettes. He tapped the package against his hand until one dangle out.

"Good morning, baby girl."

"Good morning, Daddy."

He lit the cigarette and brought it to his mouth. He inhaled, and turned his head to blow the smoke away from her face.

"Daddy, where's Gayle?"

"She's at Olivia's. I'm going to go get her as soon as I drop you off at school."

"When did she go there?"

"You don't need to worry about that. Go get ready for school."

He was clearly in no mood for small talk.

Dani tried to remember if she had heard or seen anything during the night.

She headed to the bathroom to prepare for what she knew would be a very long day at school.

CHAPTER 9

Olivia

That afternoon Reverend Ferguson, Gertrude and Olivia sat around the kitchen table. The house was quiet except for the kitchen conversation so it was easy for Gayle and Dani to listen in from their bedroom where they were sequestered.

"Daddy, maybe Gayle should come and stay with me while everyone cools down a little."

Reverend Ferguson was not sure if that was the answer, but he was sure they all could use some time to cool off.

"You know that might not be such a bad idea."

"Daniel, that's what's wrong with her now. You're always giving into her."

"You don't get a vote in this one," said Olivia.

"What about school? There are still a few weeks left before the end of school," said Gertrude.

"Daddy, I'll drive her to school every day. I promise she won't miss one day."

"What about Leonard?" asked Reverend Ferguson, "How will your husband feel about having another person in his home?"

"He suggested it. We talked about it before I left the home this morning. She will be fine, Daddy. We all know that. Why do you think she called me as soon as she left last night? She found a phone and called me."

"Well, you should have called your father immediately," said Gertrude.

"That wouldn't have done anyone any good. After all, it was late and y'all were probably asleep. Y'all did not even know she was gone. I called as soon I woke up this morning. Daddy, please, this is good for everyone."

"If you and Leonard are in agreement, why isn't he here?" asked Gertrude.

"He's subbing at Butler Elementary. They asked him to work today. Daddy, I'll have him call you as soon as he gets home."

Reverend Ferguson hesitated. He wanted to do what was best for his family.

"Okay, she can go with you, but only until the end of school year. Gayle is not your responsibility."

Olivia rose from her chair and kissed her father on the forehead.

"But she is. Remember, I promised mama."

Gertrude, who found it hard to measure against the perfect first wife and mother, took the statement as a signal to leave the room.

CHAPTER 10

Dani

Dani hurried through the meal so she could go to her room and watch the Miss Louisiana Pageant. There were no black contestants, but Dani dreamed of one day competing for the crown.

She stood on her feet and paraded around her bedroom pretending to be a contestant as she waved to the audience.

"Dani, call the ambulance … Your daddy is sick," Gertrude bellowed from the hallway.

She left her room and headed down the hall to the living room.

She could not make sense of what she saw.

Her father stooped over a chair, holding his chest.

"Get some help Dani! Get some help!" yelled Gertrude.

Dani ran to the phone to call her grandmother. Perhaps her nerves would not allow her to dial the correct number, but the phone call was unsuccessful.

I will run down to Grandmother's house. That is faster than trying to get her on the phone.

She took off running.

She could hear herself breathing.

When she reached the house, she pounded on the front door and yelled, "Grandmother! Grandmother, Daddy is sick."

Grandmother opened the door after what felt like an eternity.

"What's wrong child?"

"Daddy is sick."

"Okay baby, let me put my house shoes on. I will be right there."

The old woman turned away and walked to the back of the house.

Dani ran next door and tried to open the fence in front of Reverend Pugh's house. She yanked at the locked gate several times to no avail.

She felt alone in the dark of the night. It was quiet except for the rattling of the metal fence.

Beverly ...I will try Beverly's house.

She ran past her own house and to the front yard of the other neighbor, Beverly.

She pounded on the door.

"Beverly, Beverly, Daddy is sick!"

Beverly opened the door, shouted back into the house for someone to call an ambulance and followed Dani next door.

When the ambulance arrived, Beverly took Dani back to her front porch where the two of them sat.

"Everything will be fine," said Beverly.

She placed Dani's head in her lap and stroked her hair.

Dani stayed in the comfort of Beverly's lap until Grandmother came to get her.

CHAPTER 11

Gayle

The next morning, Gayle ran her fingers against her green and yellow plaid skirt. She adjusted the matching scarf and straightened the buttons of her shirt. She joined the rest of the family in the car and they headed to church.

Today she would tell Daddy about her new job and ask if she could stay at Olivia's throughout the summer.

In spite of everything, she missed Daddy and Dani and looked forward to seeing them every Sunday morning.

Leonard parked the family car in the parking spot next to the empty one reserved for the pastor at the back of the church.

They laughed as they made their way into the church where Sunday school was just beginning. The small edifice held all of the classes.

Leonard and Olivia strolled over to the front right side of where the married couples' class met. Gayle dropped Tasha off in the primary class and then walked toward the choir stand to her class.

She could see Deacon Loveless on the phone through the opened door to the hallway leading to the Pastor's study. He held the receiver with one hand and his head with the other.

Gayle stood there for a moment, trying to decide whether to check on Deacon Loveless or to refer the matter to Leonard. Deacon Loveless hung up the phone and yelled, "Oh Lawd, Reverend Ferguson is dead!"

A quiet wave made its way across the sanctuary.

Gayle dropped her Bible and her Sunday school book. She could not make sense of deacon's outburst.

One of the sisters made her way to Gayle and led her to the pastor's study. Leonard and Olivia followed behind.

"Let's go to the pastor's study and find out what's going on," Leonard said to Olivia in a composed voice.

Gayle was crying uncontrollably.

When they reached the Pastor's study, Olivia stood stoic with her arms around Gayle.

Leonard closed the door.

"Now, Deacon Loveless, tell us exactly what happened," said Olivia.

Even as she waited to hear the deacon's response, Gayle knew her daddy was gone.

CHAPTER 12

Dani

Later that morning, the front door of Grandmother's house swung open and Dani's eyes popped open. She jumped off her grandmother's couch.

"Mommee!"

Gertrude hugged Dani and walked over to her mother.

"Olivia ...," Dani squealed with joy when she saw her sister walk into the house.

She jumped into Olivia's arms. Dani peeped over Olivia's shoulder hoping to see her father walk through the door next. She turned to Gertrude and said, "I missed church today. Grandmother said we could stay home. But can I still go to Olivia's house?"

"Let's go home first. And then we'll talk about it," said Gertrude.

"Yes, ma'am. Where is Daddy? Is he at home?"

"Dani you go home with Gertrude and I'll be down in a minute," said Olivia.

"OK," Dani said, oblivious to the clandestine undertones from the adults.

Gertrude took Dani's hand and led her to the front door.

Dani turned to look at Olivia before walking out of the door. Olivia forced a smile and winked at her little sister.

Olivia's parked car was in the driveway.

Dani ran to Olivia's car, eager to give her father a hug and welcome him home.

He was not there.

She looked at Gertrude.

They walked to the side of the house and Gertrude unlocked the door.

"When is Daddy coming home?"

"Your daddy isn't coming home. Your daddy is dead."

"Daddy is what?"

Gertrude said nothing.

"Dead! He just had a stomachache. What do you mean he's dead?"

Gertrude shook her head slightly, and ran to her bedroom.

Dani stood in the middle of the kitchen alone.

She did not understood what "dead" meant.

Daddy had talked to her about death. He said, "When a person dies, they go to one of two places. Those who believe in Jesus go to heaven. Those who don't believe in Jesus go to hell."

Daddy believed in Jesus.

Daddy was in heaven.

How long would he be there?

When was he coming back?

Her heart began to beat fast and loud. Her eyes burned with tears.

She was unable to move.

Olivia came into the house and with one leap, Dani was in her sister's arms, holding on for dear life.

#####

In the weeks that followed Reverend Ferguson's death, tension grew between Gertrude and Olivia. Olivia wanted to spend time with her little sister. Gertrude wanted to keep Dani as far away from Olivia as possible because she was convinced that Olivia was going to take Dani and never bring her back.

Dani stayed under a protective eye at Grandmother's house while Gertrude went to work each day. Dani remained in the tiny house and could only go outside for a few minutes while Grandmother stood watching from the living room window.

Dani loved to play on the front porch. She could pretend to be anything she wanted and be anywhere she wanted with Mrs. Beasley.

"I've got to run to the bathroom Dani. Stay right there, I'll be right back, honey."

"Yes, ma'am," said Dani.

Within seconds, the white impala pulled in front of the house.

Dani smiled when she saw her sister.

Olivia got out of the car and walked toward Dani.

She knelt down eye level to her baby sister and said, "I have something for you in my car ..."

PART II

CHAPTER 13

Olivia

The six years after the death of their father brought many changes for the sisters. Olivia believed her parents would have been pleased.

Gayle finished her last year of high school and graduated Cum Laude from Grambling College. She entered and won a playwriting contest that brought her national recognitions and a job offer from television producer, Norman Lear. Olivia believed Gayle would be successful but agonized about her decision to move to New York so quickly after graduating from college.

Dani, now a freshman in high school usually made the Honor Roll but thought more about the boys in the classroom than she thought about her homework. Dani's ever-developing figure caused Olivia even more uneasiness.

But Olivia could not shake the feeling that something was not quite right about the way one of the deacons ogled Dani at church last Sunday. Olivia knew whenever the Lord gave her "that feeling" she had better keep her eyes opened because something was about to happen.

"Something about him just doesn't sit right with me," said Olivia to her husband.

"I think you're over reacting. He's never done anything to make me think he was less than honorable," said Leonard.

Olivia rolled her eyes and added creole seasoning to the chicken wings and drumsticks.

"How are you going to cook that chicken?" he asked, refilling his mason jar with water.

"I'm not going to fry it, that's for sure. You know what the doctor said."

"The doctor said I should cut back on fried foods. He didn't say that I had to eliminate them."

"And I haven't eliminated them. We had fried chicken last week, remember?"

"You bet I remember. Honey you know I love the way you cook. But a man can take only so much baked food."

"I know what you're trying to do. You're trying to change the subject."

"I'm not trying to change the subject. I just do not think we have anything to worry about when it comes to Deacon Samuels. Besides, he is a married man. I know he does not come to church as he should, but give him a break. Now fry woman fry!"

Leonard drank the rest of his iced-tea, gave Olivia a kiss on the cheek and headed for the living room.

Olivia shook her head, placed the chicken in a pan and put it in the oven. She washed and dried her hands. Then she walked into the laundry room and grabbed a stack of Leonard's clean undershirts that she had folded earlier in the day.

Olivia placed the stack of undershirts in Leonard's dresser drawer and walked over to her side of the bed. There she sat and watched Dani and Tasha as they played a game of checkers on her bedroom floor.

Olivia positioned herself across the bed.

The phone rang.

"I'll get it. Y'all keep playing," she said and reached for the phone. "Hello?"

"Hey, it's Gayle. How are you?"

"Hey Gayle, I'm fine. How are you?"

"Great. The job is going well."

"Have you thought anymore about getting a dog? I worry about you living alone in New York."

"Actually, that's what I'm calling about. I'm not living alone anymore."

"You got a dog? What kind?"

"No, I didn't get a dog."

"You didn't? Did you get a roommate? You need to be careful about strangers. Who is this person?"

"Well, it's not exactly a roommate."

"Gayle, what are you talking about? It's not a dog and it's not a roommate?"

"It's my husband. I got married."

"You did what?"

Olivia gasped in horror.

The girls stopped playing checkers.

"What do you think happened?" asked Dani.

"I don't know but Mama's not happy about it."

"Do you think we should leave the room?"

"Not until she tells us to leave. I've got to hear this."

They sat quietly, listening to Olivia's every word and watching her every gesture.

"But you moved to New York in June. It's August. Stop playing around and tell me the truth."

Olivia flailed her hands as if Gayle could see her.

"I'm not kidding. I got married. His name is William. I met him two weeks ago. When you meet him, you'll love him as much as I do."

"You know nothing about this man. For all you know he could be a serial killer!"

Olivia paced back and forth alongside her bed, pulling the telephone cord behind her.

"Who are his people?"

"His family lives in Las Vegas."

"What?"

"Olivia, I have to go. There's someone at the door."

"But we are not finished talking about this."

"I know. I'll call you back as soon as I get rid of whoever is at the door."

Olivia slammed the receiver onto the phone.

"Lord, have mercy!"

"What happened?" Dani asked.

"Gayle got married last night."

Olivia shook her head with disgust. "And she just met the man two weeks ago!"

CHAPTER 14

Gayle

Gayle took a few sips of her husband's beer after hanging up the phone with Olivia. William Baskerville was the most handsome man she had ever seen and she was crazy about him. He was smart too. He knew all there was to know about choreography. That is why Gayle chose him to be the choreographer for her Off-Broadway play. She loved to watch him work his magic on stage. Gayle was sure that Olivia would like William once she got to know him.

She looked around their small efficiency apartment. The nicely decorated one room dwelling held a green-tweed sofa bed and chair, a white modular-molded plastic bookshelf and matching coffee table. The tiny kitchenette included a miniature refrigerator, small stove and even smaller sink.

Double-glass doors spanned the length of one wall. The opposite wall held the entrance to a small bathroom and closet. She was a long way from Bossier City, where she got her start.

It was never her intent to hurt or to disappoint Olivia.

If Olivia is upset about my bringing a complete stranger into the family, Gayle thought, how is she going to react when she finds out that the complete stranger is an agnostic?

CHAPTER 15

Dani

Olivia warned the girls repeatedly about putting the family business in the streets, but Dani could not wait to share the news with her friend, Aretha.

"Aretha, guess what happened!" Dani said, throwing a pair of white canvas sneakers in the corner of the closet where she had ensconced herself. It was the only place in the house to have a private telephone conversation. Tasha was watching television in their room, adhering to the strict code of conduct that included never disturbing anyone having a closet conversation.

"What?" asked Aretha, chewing something crunchy.

"Gayle got married."

"To who? Didn't she just move to New York?"

"That's the same thing Olivia said. What are you eating?"

"Potato chips and I'm almost done. I bet Olivia had a cow."

"You just don't know. I thought she was going to reach through the phone and strangle Gayle."

They sat on the phone in silence for a minute – that is, silence plus a muffled crunching.

"I can't believe Gayle got married," said Aretha.

"I hope Jesus doesn't come back before I get married," Dani said.

"Well, I hope He doesn't come back before I get to have sex," Aretha said.

"Yeah. I want to get married and have lots of children before I die."

"I don't know if I'm going to get married. But I do know that I don't want to be running around behind a bunch of children."

"My husband is going to be tall, light-skinned and saved. He got to be saved," said Dani.

"My husband is going to have a good job. I am not going to be poor."

"At the rate I'm going, I'll never get married. Boys don't even notice when I'm in the room."

"That's because you don't talk to them."

"I don't know what to say."

"You can ask them questions. Most boys like to talk about themselves."

"Anyway, they only want one thing. And I am saving that. But for real, Aretha, let's promise to tell each other when we do it the first time."

"OK. That way the other one will know just what to expect."

"It will be our little secret, OK?"

"OK. You ready?"

"Yeah. One, two, three ...,"

Then, in unison, they promised, "Secret, secret do not tell. If you do, you'll go to hell."

CHAPTER 16

Gayle

Gayle could not control her excitement. She wore a grin as she gazed longingly at her husband who was sleeping next to her. She crawled out of bed digging her feet into thick shag carpet and started a pot of coffee. She planned to fix his favorite breakfast: vegetable and cheese omelet with a side of bacon.

"You're so beautiful," he said in his signature deep-raspy voice.

Gayle turned to see her husband using his arms to pull himself up in the bed. Her eyes affixed to the biceps bulging from his white t-shirt.

"I didn't mean to wake you. Would you like a cup of coffee?"

"Sure, thank you."

Gayle could feel her husband's eyes watching her measure the coffee and fill the bin.

She felt so beautiful and she basked in the attention.

Gayle used the lines on the coffee pot to measure the water. She and her husband were both heavy coffee drinkers so she filled the pot to capacity with water and poured it into coffee maker.

"So what are your plans for today?" asked William, never taking his eyes off his wife.

"We're pitching ideas for the show today. I am not sure how long that will take. But I plan to meet you at the studio tonight for play rehearsal. Are you hungry?"

Gayle sat on the bed next to her husband and they waited for the coffee to brew.

"I'm starving. But let me make breakfast. What would you like?" he asked.

"You want to make breakfast?"

"I sure do. My mama taught me how to cook. She said we needed to be able to take care of ourselves."

William threw his legs over the side of the bed and kissed his wife on the cheek.

"Speaking of your mother, did you tell her you got married?" asked Gayle.

"Yes, I did. She can't wait to meet you."

"She didn't get upset when she found out how long we'd known each other?"

Gayle walked over to the kitchenette and poured two cups of coffee. She handed a cup to William. She walked over to the double glass doors, opened the drapes and revealed a pair of sheers. Soon the room reflected the light and airy mood of the couple.

"No, mom's cool as long as I stay out of jail and out of her pockets. She got really excited when I told her you were from Louisiana."

"Really? What did she say?"

"Gumbo, Etouffée and Jambalaya!"

William wrapped his arms around his bride.

"Well, Olivia wasn't as receptive as your mother," said Gayle turning to face him.

"She wasn't? What did she say?"

"Who is he? Who are his people? And how do you know he's not a serial killer?"

"What did she say when you told her that I wasn't sure about this God thing?

"I didn't exactly get around to telling her that part yet."

"Your father was a minister, right?"

"He sure was."

"And he was the pastor at your church, right?"

"That's right."

"And you come from a church every Sunday kind of family, right?"

"Right again."

"Are you sure you can handle this?

"I'm sure. You married me and not my family."

"But your family is important to you. And I am now a part of that family. You have to tell them."

"I will. But right now I have to get dressed for work."

She took another sip of coffee and headed for the bathroom.

"I'll be out in a few minutes," she said looking back at her husband.

"OK. Breakfast will be waiting."

Gayle entered the bathroom and closed the door. She looked at her image in the mirror and wondered whether she had made the right decision.

Gayle and William moved to Bossier City at the end of Dani's first year in high school. Gayle loved her work in the big city but missed the small town feel that Bossier offered. She continued to work as a freelance writer and planned to travel back and forth to New York when necessary.

The couple had been married over a year, but this was the first time the family had the pleasure of meeting Mr. William Baskerville. Olivia was still upset over the surprise marriage and she still did not know about his religious persuasion or lack thereof.

"Hello, my name is William. I'm pleased to meet you," the short, toffee-colored stranger with a deep James Earl Jones voice introduced himself. He wore khaki pants and an opened khaki vest on top of a basic white t-shirt.

Olivia shook the hand of the man who had stolen the heart of her young sister.

Mama Bear was reserved but cordial.

"I'm Olivia Johnson, pleased to meet you, too."

The Ferguson family confirmation hearing commenced in the living room. Everyone wanted to glean information from the bushy-haired stranger. The lovebirds held hands on the couch. A smile from ear to ear covered Gayle's face as she presented William like a vacation souvenir. Tasha and Dani sat together on the love seat and Leonard sat in his Lazy-Boy recliner.

Olivia pretended to be busy in the kitchen.

"So where are you from, son?" Leonard asked.

"Las Vegas, sir."

He is very respectful. He will earn a few points for that.

"What kind of work do you do?" asked Leonard.

"I'm an actor/choreographer. That's how I met Gayle," he said smiling at his wife.

"How do you plan on supporting your wife in Bossier? There's not a lot of work for actors and choreographers in this area," said Leonard.

William leaned back in his seat and crossed his left leg over his right knee.

"I plan on teaching in one of the schools."

"Teaching what, son? Did you go to school to learn how to be a teacher?"

William released Gayle's hand, crossed his arms and cleared his throat.

Gayle jumped in, "We have a few leads. William knows production and lighting. We are positive that something will come through. And besides, I'm still writing for television."

Strike one.

"Where do you go to church?" Olivia asked.

Gayle had prepared William for this question.

"I have to admit that I haven't been in a while," he said with a chuckle.

Strike Two.

The native Las Vegan remained cool as the family bombarded him with questions. He was poised and almost appeared to find it all very entertaining.

William was positive that he had won them over with his charisma.

He was in for a rude awakening.

CHAPTER 17

Gayle

Gayle was not in the mood for unsolicited advice so she skipped Sunday dinner at Olivia's house. It was hard enough going to church without her husband and she did not want to hear what Olivia had to say about his absence from church. This was the third Sunday in a row William missed church service. He had been in such a slump lately. He had been unsuccessful at finding work and some mornings he had not even bother to get dressed.

All I want is for him to make an effort to go to church, Gayle thought. Daddy always went to church. Leonard goes every Sunday. That is what husbands are supposed to do – take their wives and families to church. I just want to share my love for God with the man that I love.

"So how was service?" asked William as soon as Gayle walked in the door. He was on the couch still in his pajamas watching television with his feet on the table and his hand in a bag of Lays potato chips.

"It was good."

She walked past him and headed to the bedroom where she quickly relieved her feet of the four-inch platform shoes.

"Did the preacher tell everyone how they were doomed for hell?"

Gayle ignored the sarcasm.

"What's wrong?" he asked, following her into the bedroom.

I hate it when he pretends he does not know what's wrong with me.

William put his arms around his wife. She loved how she could feel his muscles pressing up against her. He smelled of Jergens lotion, potato chips and Budweiser.

Her anger began to melt with the touch of his hands.

"Gayle, when you married me I wasn't going to church every Sunday and I'm not going to start now. You're just mad because Olivia probably said something about me missing church."

"It's not about Olivia. It's about having a relationship with Christ."

"Don't start preaching to me," he said walking away.

"Don't walk away," said Gayle, "can't we at least talk about it?"

Gayle followed her husband into the living room where he reattached himself to the couch.

They sat looking in each other's eyes for a few minutes.

The phone rang.

It was a welcomed intrusion.

Gayle picked up the receiver.

"Hello?"

"Hey, Gayle. It's Dani."

"Dani, what's up?"

"Mrs. Clemente, the drama teacher at school asked me to give you a message. I was going to give it to you when you came over for dinner, but you didn't come."

"Yeah, I wanted to come home and lay down for a few minutes. What's the message?"

"We're getting ready for our annual school production and she wanted to know if William would be willing to help with the choreography. I told her I'd pass the message along."

"Dani, that's good news. Thanks. How do I get in touch with her?"

"She said for you to call the school tomorrow around two o'clock."

"OK. Now how would you feel about having William working at your school? It won't be uncool or anything, will it?"

"It won't bother me."

"OK, I'll talk to you later. Love you."

"Love you too. Bye."

Gayle hung up the phone and turned to her husband who was now half-asleep.

"William," she said stirring him from his rest, "that was Dani on the phone. Parkway is doing a production and they want you to help with the choreography."

"Really?"

He smiled.

"Yes, isn't that great. Mrs. Clemente wants you to call the school on tomorrow around two o'clock."

Gayle thanked God for the pleasant surprise.

It was not about the money for her. She earned more than enough income from her writing. It was about making her husband happy.

"You just don't know. It's been so hard to find work down here."

Gayle scooted closer to her husband.

She placed his hand in hers.

"That's only because they don't know how good you are. This will be the start of something big. You watch and see when people start to hear about William Baskerville, there'll be more than enough work."

"Thanks, honey."

William pulled Gayle into his arms.

"Listen, let's not fight. I promise to go to church next Sunday, but if somebody tries to lay hands on me, I'm going to lay my fist across their face."

CHAPTER 18

Dani

Dani stood at the entrance of the sophomore hallway, wondering if this would be the year she found a boyfriend. Her spectrum of friends ran the gamut of high school social groups. She had black friends, white friends, hip friends and not-so-hip friends.

It was a typical Louisiana fall morning. The grass was still wet with the morning dew. The sound of planes landing and taking off ricocheted from the nearby Air Force base. The roar of passing cars rand out as commuters made their way to work.

Dani watched as Romeo Jones and his friends poured out of his candy-red Ford Mustang. Romeo played basketball and football and usually earned a spot on the honor roll. His father was an Air Force officer stationed at Barksdale Air Force Base. His sporty two-door coupe, with white vinyl interior usually contained sweaty-adolescent ballplayers and he was headed in Dani's direction. She grabbed her wallet and pretended to peruse a few of the pictures inside: Olivia and Leonard standing by the fireplace on Christmas morning, Aretha and her homecoming date from last year, and Tasha's school picture from last year.

When Dani looked up, Romeo was standing in front of her.

She could not figure out what to do with her hands.

Romeo wore bell-bottom jeans and a Parkway Panther football jersey. The red-nylon jersey with a large number twenty-seven printed on front complemented his broad shoulders. Parkway was scheduled to play that night, and the football players wore their jerseys to school for the pep rally.

Romeo's shoulders seemed to go on forever.

"You're Dani, right?"

She swallowed a big chunk of air and twisted a lock of hair around her finger.

"Yes," she purred, dumbfounded because he knew her name.

"Hi. I'm Romeo."

He smiled, exposing a perfect set of teeth. Dani thought she saw a sparkle in the corner of his upper front tooth.

"I know you are." *That was a stupid thing to say.*

"So, Dani, do you have a boyfriend?"

She swallowed again, triggering an irrepressible cough.

She covered her mouth.

"No," she said, fighting the urge to cough again.

She glanced around the campus with the hope that someone was watching Romeo Jones talking to Dani Ferguson.

"Has anyone asked you to the homecoming dance?" he asked.

Did he just ask me what I think he asked me?

"Um ... I mean, no."

Dani gained control over the tickle in her throat.

"Would you like to go with me?"

"Would I like to go with you? I guess so. I mean ... sure. Yes, OK."

She answered quickly, before he had a chance to change his mind.

"Cool. Let's talk later. I'd better get to class," he said darting to the senior hall.

He smiled again, and this time Dani was sure there was a sparkle.

The tardy bell rang.

Oh no, I am late.

Dani took off as quickly as possible for class, stuffing the pictures and wallet back into her purse.

#####

After school, Dani sat in the closet holding her knees to her chest with one hand and holding the phone to her ear with the other. She could not wait to hear Aretha's response when she told her about Romeo Jones.

"Guess what?"

"What?"

"You're never going to believe what happened to me today at school!"

"Girl, stop playing around and tell me what happened."

"I got asked to the homecoming dance," Dani said with a squeal, pounding her feet against the floor.

"You did? Who asked you?"

"Romeo Jones. You do not know him. He is a senior, plays basketball and football. He's cute, has a beautiful afro and a red Mustang."

Dani squealed again. This time standing to her feet and waving her hands in the air.

"Were you nervous talking to him?"

"You know I was."

Dani returned to her seated position, breathless and excited.

"I can't believe it, girl. You're going to homecoming."

"Hold on, I didn't say I was going. I said I was asked."

"What are you talking about?"

"I still have to get permission from Olivia."

"I hope she lets you go. Have you thought about what you are going to wear?"

"I'll probably have to borrow a dress from you."

"That's cool."

"There's just one problem," said Dani.

"What's the problem?"

"I kind of already told Romeo I'd go with him. So Olivia *has* to let me go, or I don't know what I'm going to do."

"Why did you tell him you would go? You should have said you would let him know. Boys like it when you play hard to get."

"I don't know. I have never been asked to go anywhere before. He caught me off guard, and before I even thought about it, I told him I'd go."

"What if Olivia says you can't go? What are you going to do?"

"I don't know … let's just pray that she gives me permission."

#####

That night Dani stood in the mirror practicing her presentation. She knew Olivia would have many questions about Romeo and she planned to have an answer for each of them. The dance was a few weeks away and there was little time left to prepare.

She will want to know about Romeo's parents. His dad is in the Air Force. They just moved here a few years ago, and they probably go to church on base.

She will want to know how I plan to get a dress for the dance. I will borrow one from Aretha and it will not cost a thing.

She will want to know more about the dance. It is from eight to eleven, so I will be home early.

Romeo has his own car, so she will not have to take us. The only thing she does not need to know is that Romeo drives a red mustang. It is probably best to keep that bit of information to myself.

Dani headed to Olivia's room armed with information. She stood in the doorway, a bit afraid to enter, and even more afraid to broach the volatile subject.

An earth-toned quilt and topped with matching pillow shams covered the king-sized bed. It sat between two windows. A wooden nightstand with brown porcelain lamps lay below each window.

Olivia smiled when she saw Dani. "Hey, Dani, come on in."

Dani entered the room and lay down next to Olivia on the bed.

The room smelled of Estee Lauder Youth Dew and evoked a sense of calm.

Rockford Files was on television.

Olivia yawned.

"Are you tired?" Dani asked.

"A little. What's up?"

"Well, the homecoming dance is coming up at school."

Dani paused, waiting for a reaction.

There was none.

"Anyway, this boy asked me to go with him."

Olivia sat up and positioned her back against the headboard.

"Would you turn the TV down?" she asked, pointing in the direction of the chest of drawers where the small TV sat.

Dani walked over to the TV and turned the knob to lower the volume. She sat on the bed, facing Olivia. She could see Olivia's face through the flashes of light from the television.

"So, who is this boy?"

"His name is Romeo … Romeo Jones."

"Romeo? Is that his real name?" asked Olivia while laughing.

"Yes, ma'am."

"Well, who is this Romeo Jones? Who are his people?"

"His daddy is in the Air Force. They're stationed at the base."

"How old is this Romeo?"

"I don't know, but he's a senior."

"A senior? Baby, you're too young to be going somewhere with a boy that old."

Dani had not anticipated Olivia would have a problem with Romeo's age.

Her top lip began to tremble and droop.

She willed herself not to cry.

"Yes, ma'am," she responded.

Dani bit her bottom lip and slowed her breathing. She walked over to the television and turned up the volume.

She returned to her room and burst out in tears.

After a few minutes, Dani pulled herself together enough to drag the phone into the closet and call Aretha.

"I can't go."

"You can't go where?"

"I can't go to the homecoming dance. Olivia said 'no.'"

"You're kidding me."

"She thinks he's too old."

"So you can't go because he's too old? That does not make sense. What does his age have to do with it? And how does she know how old he is anyway?"

"I told her he was a senior."

"Why?"

"Because she asked me."

"So did she say that you couldn't go to homecoming or that you couldn't go to homecoming with Romeo?"

"She said that I was too young to go with a boy that old."

"So you can go to homecoming, just not with Romeo?"

"What difference does it make? I'm not going."

"All you have to do is meet Romeo at the dance. You'll still be his date for the dance; he just won't pick you up."

"Aretha, I don't know. Olivia will probably figure it out, and then I'll be in really big trouble."

"How's she going to find out? I'm not telling her, are you?"

"No. But what if …?"

"When is the dance?"

"Saturday after next."

"OK. Just wait a few days and then ask if you can spend the night at my house on the night of the dance. I will get my cousin to drive us to the dance. It'll be fun."

"What about your mother? She will see us getting all dressed up. What if she says something to Olivia?"

"Mama will be doing what she does every Saturday night. She will be in her bed watching TV or working on her second job. She won't know and she won't care."

"Aretha, I'm not sure about this."

"Just think about it. If you change your mind, we do not have to go. We'll just stay at my house and watch TV."

" OK, let me think about it. I'll call you later."

"Promise me that you'll think about it."

"I promise."

"Good. I'll talk to you later, Bye."

"Bye."

Dani had a decision to make.

#####

Dani sat on the floor outside of her homeroom class the next day with a group of other students stenciling letters that would spell out P-A-N-T-H-E-R-S for the Homecoming door-decorating contest. She listened as the other girls talked about dresses, hairstyles, shoes, dates, and so on in anticipation of the upcoming dance.

Dani thought, how am I going to tell Romeo that I cannot go to the dance with him? Should I apologize and say that my sister will not allow me to date upperclassmen. No, that will probably lead to other questions about why my sister is calling telling me what I can and cannot do.

A group of football players came from the library and down the hall, straight for Dani and her classmates. Everyone watched as if it were the Changing of the Guard at Buckingham Palace. The quartet basked in the glow of the attention of the onlookers. Dani recognized Romeo among the four and thought it was as good a time as any to break the news to him.

"Hey," he said withdrawing from the group, and walking toward Dani.

"Hey," she murmured.

She could feel the eyes of every one of her classmates watching.

"You got a minute?" she asked.

"Sure. Hey man, I'll catch you later," said Romeo to one of his friends.

"Let's talk over there."

He pointed in the direction of the water fountain down the hall.

Dani and Romeo walked to the water fountain and Romeo leaned over for a sip.

"What's up?" he asked, wiping his mouth and looking into Dani's eyes.

She combed the hallway with her eyes.

Her feet found an impromptu beat.

"I'm really sorry, but uh... I uh, I can't go to the dance with you."

"Oh,yeah? Why not?"

He seemed unruffled but surprised as if finding another date would be a minor inconvenience.

"Well, I mean I can't ride to the dance with you, but I can meet you there."

"That's cool."

"OK."

"By the way, your homeroom door looks good. You guys will probably win."

"Thanks."

"Well, I gotta go catch up with my boys. See ya' around."

Romeo turned and walked away.

That was easier than Dani anticipated. The hard part was going to be pulling it off without Olivia finding out.

CHAPTER 19

Gayle

Gayle typed her address on her cover page and turned the knob until the paper ejected from her electric typewriter. She had completed her manuscript two weeks before the deadline and things could not be better. William was busy with Parkway's production of *The Music Man*, and he had even gone to church with her every Sunday since he began working on the choreography.

"Hey, honey. You still pecking on that thing?" said William after entering the house.

Gayle looked at the kitchen clock. It was later than she thought.

"You kept the kids after school a long time, it's almost seven."

"Nope, I wasn't at the school."

"Where were you?"

"I went out for a couple of drinks after rehearsal. I don't know if I want to do the production anyway."

"You're thinking about quitting?"

"They're not paying me enough. I'm worth more than what they have to offer."

"You're worth more than that? It is a job, William. It's the first thing you've been offered since we moved here."

"So I'll find something else."

"How? You did not even look for this one. You can't find a job sitting around the house all day."

"Look, I'm not cut out for a nine to five," said William as he turned and headed out of the door.

"Where are you going?"

He did not reply.

"William, where are you going?"

He answered with a slam of the door.

CHAPTER 20

Dani

The night of the homecoming dance, Dani packed for an overnight stay at Aretha's house.

"Dani, let's go," yelled Olivia from the hallway, "We need to leave now so I can drop you off at Aretha's and get back in time to start cooking."

"Yes, ma'am. I'm coming."

Dani grabbed her purse and her overnight bag.

"I know what you're up to," said Tasha, tapping Dani on the shoulder.

"What are you talking about?" she asked, stopping in her tracks.

"You're just trying to get out of helping with dinner tonight. Now I'm going to have to cut up all the vegetables and clean up by myself."

Tasha playfully tapped Dani again, this time a little harder.

Dani could not let Tasha get away with the last hit, so she dropped her overnight bag on the couch and swung her purse at Tasha.

"You're in for it now," said Tasha.

She chased Dani out of the living room, through the kitchen, through the washroom and into the car. Dani locked herself in the car so Tasha could not get the last hit.

Tasha stood in the garage laughing until Olivia came out and got into the car. Tasha waved as they drove off.

#####

Aretha was waiting on her front porch wearing a pair of blue jean overalls and a white t-shirt.

Olivia parked the car and rolled her window down.

Dani opened the door and got out of the car.

"Hey, Aretha," said Olivia.

"Hi, Mrs. Olivia."

"Is your mom at home?"

"No ma'am, she hasn't made it home yet."

"OK. Y'all have fun and tell your mom I said hi."

"Yes, ma'am."

"Bye, Olivia," Dani said, "Thanks for letting me spend the night."

"OK, Dani, just be on time for Sunday school tomorrow."

CHAPTER 21

Gayle

Gayle reached for the key underneath the flowerpot on Olivia's front porch and went inside. She wanted to talk to Olivia about the change in William's behavior. Only a week ago, William slammed out of the house and did not return until just before midnight reeking of alcohol and cigarette smoke. .

Olivia was surprised to find Gayle sitting at the dining room table when she returned home from dropping Dani at Aretha's house.

"Hey Gayle, what are you doing here?"

"Hey Olivia, I just thought I'd stop by to check on Dani. Tonight was the homecoming dance, right?"

Gayle wanted to ease into the conversation about William.

"Yeah, but she went over to Aretha's. She's spending the night."

Olivia went to the sink and washed her hands. Then she pulled a bunch of turnip greens out of the refrigerator and placed them in a bowl.

"Is everything alright?" asked Olivia.

"Yeah, do you need some help?"

"I sure do. If you clean these greens, I can start on the cake."

Gayle washed her hands at the sink and Olivia pulled out the hand held electric mixer.

"Where's everybody else?" asked Gayle.

".Tasha's down the street at a friend's house and Leonard's in the back somewhere. Where's William?"

Olivia pulled a carton of eggs and a gallon of milk from the refrigerator. Then she grabbed the sugar, flour and other dry ingredients from the pantry.

"I don't know. We had a fight."

Gayle filled one side of the sink with water. She dumped the greens in the water.

"All couples fight, honey?"

Olivia turned the mixer to its lowest setting and slowly mixed dry ingredients together.

Gayle took a deep breath. She was not ready to hear Olivia say I told you so, but she did not know where else to turn. She continued cleaning the greens avoiding all eye contact with Olivia.

"I know you think we got married too fast. But we were in love. I mean I still love him. I'm just not sure I want to be married anymore."

"No matter how long you know the person before you decide to get married, there will be hard times. It is just that the longer you know a person, the more you get to know about him or her. Did something happen to make you question the way you feel?"

Gayle looked off into the distance.

"Look there's only one thing that I can think of that would make you mad enough to come over here with an overnight bag," said Olivia glancing at the couch.

"What overnight bag? I didn't bring an overnight bag."

"Then what is that?" asked Olivia, pointing to the bag on the couch.

"That's not mine."

Olivia thought for a minute.

"It must be Dani's. I've got to run it back over to her so she'll have clothes for church tomorrow."

"I'll take it to her when I finish the greens."

"Thanks. So what did William do to make you mad?"

"He wants to quit his job on the school production."

Olivia could feel her blood beginning to boil. She did not want to lose control, but if William walked in the house any time soon he would walk out with a black eye.

"Did he say why he wanted to quit?"

"Olivia, I don't think I'm ready to talk about this. I'm going to take this bag over to Aretha's."

"I'm not trying to get in your business, Gayle. You brought it up. We don't have to talk about it unless you want to."

For the next few minutes, only the sound of turnip greens splashing in and out of the water and the hum of the electric mixer could be heard.

"Was Dani upset about not going to the dance?" asked Gayle.

"Not really. She seemed fine after I said she could spend the night at Aretha's."

"I was going to take her to the mall since she couldn't go to the dance."

"I know you feel sorry for her, but that boy was just too old."

"Olivia, don't you remember what it felt like to be that age?"

"I sure do. And I remember getting whoopings behind some nappy headed boy too."

"Not you Olivia."

"Yeah girl, I haven't been saved all my life."

The air in the room grew lighter as they shared a laugh.

"I know that I can be a little overprotective at times. It is just that even if a little girl does things that are very innocent and a young man could take it the wrong way. I don't want to put Dani or Tasha in that situation."

Olivia stared into space. Lost in a lingering thought, she loosened her grip on the mixer and the batter went flying everywhere.

"Shoot, now I have to start all over," said Olivia.

"It's OK. I'll help."

"If you really want to help, run that bag over to Dani," said Olivia.

"Are you sure? I can stay longer."

"No, Gayle. Just take that to Dani and I'll see you tomorrow."

CHAPTER 22

Dani

Dani stood at the foot of Aretha's bed admiring the display of beautiful dresses.

"We have to hurry and get dressed. I pulled out three dresses. You pick the one you want to wear and I'll wear one of the others," said Aretha.

"Oh, Aretha, these are so pretty."

"Thank you. Which one do you like the best?"

Dani picked up the first one and admired the A-line, tea-length sleeveless party dress. It was navy-blue with a satin white sash.

"You wore this one to homecoming last year."

"Yeah."

"I remember because I still have the picture in my wallet."

"Yeah, but this year you'll be able to have your own homecoming pictures."

"I don't know about taking pictures. All I need is for Olivia to accidently come across one of those pictures."

"But everybody takes homecoming pictures. It is a rite of passage. You have to do it."

"Not me. Should I try this one on or should I pick the one I like the best first?"

"I think you should decide which one you like best and then try that one on. We don't have a lot of time."

Dani picked up the cobalt blue dress with the sweetheart neckline and dropped-waist tiered skirt.

"I'll probably be more comfortable in this one."

"Why? Wait do not tell me. It's because it has sleeves."

"Yeah."

"I knew it."

"But this one ..." Dani turned her attention to the third dress. It had a black-polyester bodice and silver-polyester skirt, and a sparkling rhinestone belt.

"You're so lucky. You mother lets you do whatever you want to do. How many dresses do you have?

"I don't know how lucky I am. Some days I do not even see Mama. She works two jobs and when she's home, she is usually asleep. Like tonight, Mama will not get home until late. We will be back from the dance and fast asleep before she gets home. She'll never know we were gone."

"You mean she's not on her way home from work?"

"No."

"But you told Olivia ..."

"I told Olivia that she wasn't home from work yet and she's not."

"You know Olivia wouldn't have let me spend the night if she knew that you mom was working late."

"I know. But Olivia didn't ask me if she was going to be working late."

"And you didn't tell her."

They gave each other a high five and a smile.

Aretha's cousin pulled into Parkway's crowded parking lot.

"See ya later, Cuz. Thanks for the ride. I'll call you when we're ready for you to come get us," said Aretha.

"Yeah, just don't forget my gas money."

"I won't. We'll have it for you when you come get us."

The twenty-year-old high school dropout revved his engine and raced out of the parking lot. Dani wondered how he could afford to have a car since he did not have a job, but she was smart enough not to ask questions.

A long, black banner with silver lettering hung across the outside of the girls' gym. It read, "Stairway to Heaven."

The gym set the mood for an enchanted evening with stars dangling from the ceiling among strings of white lights. The stage was set with a black-metallic backdrop and a twinkle-star archway.

"Just relax, you look like you are scared to death," said Aretha.

"I am."

"I know you are but you don't have to look like you are."

"What if we get caught?"

"What if we *don't* get caught? What if you miss all of the fun because you're worried about getting caught?"

"I guess you're right."

"Do you see Romeo anywhere?"

Dani looked around the room. She saw many familiar faces but none attached to Romeo Jones.

"No, I guess he hasn't gotten here yet."

"Good, we have time to run to the bathroom. Where is it?"

"It's in the lobby to the right."

"Let's go."

They walked past a herd of students and into the lobby. Dani searched the lobby for Romeo but another familiar face caught her eyes. There in the middle of the lobby, dressed in a pair of jeans and a Grambling Tigers sweatshirt was Gayle.

"What have you two gotten yourselves into?" she said.

Gayle did not look happy.

Aretha looked as frightened as Dani felt.

"Just walk out quietly and get in the car," said Gayle.

The three of them walked out together. Aretha got in the back seat of the car and closed the door. Dani opened the front passenger door and got in but not before moving her overnight bag from the passenger seat. Gayle got into the drivers' side.

"Olivia asked me to bring your bag to Aretha's house. Evidently, you left it on the couch and Olivia was worried that you would not have clothes for church tomorrow.

Boy was I surprised when I got to Aretha's house and her cousin told me that he just dropped you guys off at the dance. But what is really ironic is that I came over to Olivia's to take you shopping because I knew you were bummed out about the dance."

Dani did not know what to say.

"Look," she continued, "it wasn't too long ago when I was your age. And I watched as the other kids got to do the things that I was not allowed to do. So I understand what you are going through. And any crazy thing you have done that involves a boy, I've already done it."

Both Aretha and Dani cracked a smile.

"Dani, what if Olivia had been the one to drop your clothes off?" asked Gayle.

"I know."

"Don't be in such a hurry to grow up. You will be off to college in a few years and you will have more freedom than you need. Believe me, I know."

Then Gayle turned toward the back seat.

"Aretha I love you like a sister, but I can't sit back and watch you lead Dani down the wrong path."

Aretha rolled her eyes.

"Does your mother know anything about this?"

"No, she had to work."

"OK, then let's get you guys back to the house before anyone else finds out."

#####

Dani was sure God was going to punish her for sneaking off to the homecoming dance.

She made herself sick with guilt and she was not sure if she would make it to the end of the sermon as she sat in church the next day. She excused herself to go to the bathroom. She scurried down the hall, out of the exterior door and around the building to the one bathroom located in the vestibule.

The pastor was still preaching when she made her way back around the building.

"Hey, pretty lady," a voice called from the other end of the hall.

Deacon Samuels stood at the end of the hall with his hands in his pockets. His shiny black three-piece suit seemed more appropriate for a night out on the town than a Sunday morning service. He wore a fresh haircut and plenty of Old Spice cologne. The one-inch gap between his two front teeth stood out when he smiled.

Dani smiled and waited for the usher to open the door.

Samuels moved in closer.

He stood right behind her.

He was so close she could feel his breath against the back of her neck.

The usher opened the door and Dani felt a hand brush against her backside.

She stood motionless.

The gray-haired usher gestured for Dani to move.

"Come on in, baby," she said. "It's time to take the offering."

Dani made her way to the choir stand and sat next to Aretha.

"What's wrong with you?"

"Nothing. Why?"

"You look funny. Do you feel all right?"

"No, not really."

"Well, you don't look good. Do you want me to get Olivia?"

Dani closed her eyes and replayed the scene in her head. She opened her eyes to see Samuels on the front row staring straight at her.

"Do you want me to get Olivia?"

"No."

Dani was afraid to tell Olivia, and that was bad enough. But the way Samuels was looking at her gave her an uneasiness that traveled throughout her entire body.

PART III

CHAPTER 23

Dani

One month later, on Dani's sixteenth birthday, Olivia drove her to the Department of Motor Vehicle.

Dani sat in the passenger seat staring out of the window and biting her nails. *You cannot pass the car in front of you if there are double yellow lines ... I have to slow down if there is a yield sign.*

"Relax Dani," said Olivia reaching over and patting Dani on the thigh. "I think you're ready to take the test. You've practiced driving and parking, and you've studied your handbook, right?"

"Yes ma'am."

"And you've prayed about it, right?"

"Yes ma'am."

"Then don't worry about it. Just go in there and do your best. You'll be fine."

One hour later Dani walked into the house where her family was waiting with cake and ice cream in celebration of her sixteenth birthday. Leonard, Tasha, Gayle, William and even Aretha greeted her with the Happy Birthday song and a chocolate cake.

Dani blew out her candles.

"Thank you everybody."

Then she held up her license and yelled, "I got it! I got my license!"

Gayle gave Dani a hug.

Tasha gave her a high five.

"Now we don't have to worry about finding a ride to the parties on the weekends," said Aretha.

Gayle looked at Aretha and rolled her eyes.

"I'm just kidding."

"Dani, why don't you open presents and then you can cut the cake," said Gayle, cooling down what could have been a heated moment.

Dani spied two beautifully wrapped boxes sitting in one of the empty seats. One was large with shiny purple wrapping and a large white bow. Next to that box was a smaller box, wrapped in red and white leftover Christmas paper.

Leonard reached for the smaller box and handed it to Dani.

"Here open this one first. It's from me and Olivia."

Dani could not decide if she was happier about opening her present or about seeing Leonard in a playful mood. She took the small box and shook it before removing the paper.

Inside of the box was a single key.

"What's this?" asked a confused Dani.

"It's the key to your car," blurted Olivia.

Dani screamed and ran outside where she found a bright orange Chevrolet Vega. She practically knocked Leonard and Olivia over trying to hug them and thank them for the car.

"It's not new but it's new to you," said Olivia trying to regain her balance.

"Thank you. Thank you. Wait, this car was not here when we drove up. How did it get here?"

"It was parked at Rick's house across the street. I dropped an extra key off at his house. When he saw my car in the driveway, he brought your car over," said Olivia.

"Take it for a spin around the block," said Leonard.

"Will you and Olivia come with me?"

"No, take Tasha and Aretha with you. Come right back so you can finish opening your presents," said Olivia.

Dani got behind the drivers' seat. Tasha jumped into the front seat before Aretha who settled for the back seat.

Dani carefully backed out of the driveway and drove slowly down the street until she was no longer under the watchful eyes of Leonard and Olivia.

"Now put the pedal to the medal," said Aretha.

"Yeah," said Tasha.

"Y'all are not getting me in trouble. I cannot believe I got a car for my birthday. How long have y'all known I was going to get a car?"

"Mama told me this morning before y'all left to go to the DMV."

"I didn't know until Gayle told me today," said Aretha.

"How'd you get here anyway? You couldn't have told me you were coming."

Dani slowed down at the stop sign. She looked both ways and made a left turn.

"I didn't know I was coming until Gayle called me this morning. That's when she told me about the car," said Aretha.

"Now we don't have to ride the bus to school anymore," said Tasha.

"And nobody has to drop us off at church or at the games," said Dani.

"And you can drive yourself to my house and other places," said Aretha.

Tasha turned on the radio and scanned through the stations until she heard K C and the Sunshine Band singing *That's the way I like it*. Tasha turned up the volume and the girls sang along with the radio.

"Let's go get some cake," said Dani as she pulled the car into the driveway.

She placed the gear in park and turned off the ignition. The girls exited the car and scurried inside the house.

"How was it?" asked Leonard.

"Great! I love it," said Dani.

"Now it's time to open our gift. This is from me and Williami," said Gayle.

She handed Dani the gift-wrapped in purple.

Dani tore opened the box and found a set of plastic-black car mats from William and Gayle.

"Thanks guys."

She gave her sister and brother-in-law a hug.

Dani opened a card from Tasha and one from Aretha. She saw a third card sitting on the table.

"Who is this one from?" she asked.

"We're not sure. It came in the mail today. There's no return address."

Dani grabbed the card.

I wonder who is trying to play a trick on me now, she thought. There is probably some cash or something in it.

Dani opened the card and searched for the signature but there was none.

"Who's it from?" asked Aretha.

Dani looked up to find everyone looking at her waiting for the answer to the million-dollar question.

She did not know what to say.

The card had no signature, but it had Deacon Samuels written all over it.

CHAPTER 24

Dani

Dani wore a sky blue wrap skirt with a Velcro closing and matching top on the first day of school. Being a member of the junior class automatically elevated her on the popularity scale and she earned a few extra points because she did not have to ride the bus to school. She was ready to show off her new car when the unthinkable happened.

Romeo pulled up beside her in his candy-red Camaro. He honked his horn and drove away. She was glad that the two of them had remained friends after the incident at homecoming last year. Dani knew she would never be more than a friend to Romeo and that was fine with her.

Dani and Tasha looked at each other and giggled.

"Honk your horn back at him," said Tasha.

Dani pressed the car horn and blew at Romeo who was now a few feet ahead of her in traffic. But when she released her hand, the horn did not stop honking.

It was stuck.

Dani banged her fist on the steering wheel a few times trying to silence the blare all the while trying to make sure no one from school recognized her. Tasha ducked under the dashboard in the front seat.

Finally, Dani pulled over to the shoulder. She began to panic.

"I don't know how to make it stop," Dani said, hoping Tasha could come up with a remedy.

Tasha crawled up from her hiding place.

But she had nothing to offer.

"People are laughing at us," Dani said, sinking deeper into the seat.

"I know. I wish it wasn't so loud," said Tasha, yelling over the noise.

"Let's go back home and see if Olivia can make it stop."

"What?" asked Tasha.

"Let's go back," she yelled, gesturing in the direction of the house.

"You mean you want to drive back home with the horn blowing like this?"

"What choice do we have?"

Dani merged into the traffic, turned around at the nearest intersection and drove the half mile back home like an emergency vehicle with a loud siren. She parked the car in the driveway and the girls ran to the front door with the horn still blowing. Tasha tried to open the door. It was locked. With the keys still in her hand, she quickly entered with her house key.

The lights were out and the house was quiet.

There was no sign of Olivia.

"She must be in the bed," said Tasha.

They tiptoed to the back of the house and headed to the master bedroom.

They slowly opened the door.

Heavy drapes darkened the room and it was difficult to see.

"Olivia," said Dani, just above a whisper.

What happened next brought the three of them to their knees.

CHAPTER 25

Olivia

Olivia arrived home that morning after working the overnight shift and began helping her family get their day started.

"I put some of the leftovers and a couple of pieces of cake in your lunch for you," she had said to Leonard before he left for work.

"Y'all have a good day," she said, practically pushing her family out of the door.

Olivia enjoyed a cup of coffee and prepared to spend some time in prayer. She locked the exterior doors and turned off the lights in the house before heading to her bedroom. She closed the drapes and turned off the television and anything else that could become a distraction before kneeling down next to her bed to pray.

"Dear Lord, You are worthy of all praise, all honor and all glory. There is no other like You in all of the earth. You are the beginning, the end, the alpha and the omega. Father, I ask You to forgive me of my sins and to create in me a clean heart. Lord, I invite You into my heart and into my home. Father, please come into this house …."

It was at that very moment that Olivia heard the bedroom door open and someone whisper her name.

She turned toward the door.

The darkened room distorted her vision. All she could see was the silhouette of a figure standing at the door. Olivia assumed her prayer was answered and that Jesus had entered the house.

At first, she was unable to speak at all.

Then she screamed.

Her eyes grew wide; she grabbed her chest and fell backwards onto the floor.

When Tasha and Dani heard her scream, they responded with their own screams.

The dueling shrieks went on for almost a minute.

Finally, they realized that they had frightened each other and everyone began laughing.

Loud.

Uncontrollable.

Tear jerking.

Hold-on-to-your-stomach-laughter.

Got to-stop-for-air-laughter.

At some point, Tasha turned on the lights.

They looked at each other and began laughing all over again.

That day Dani learned two valuable lessons.

She learned that Olivia had a very special relationship with God.

She learned that Olivia prayed even when no one was watching, and she prayed with the expectation that God would answer.

Dani believed if Olivia had this kind of relationship with God it would only be a matter of time before God told Olivia about Deacon Samuels.

CHAPTER 26

Gayle

The distress in her marriage began to take a toll on Gayle. She was so agitated that she walked into Brookshire's grocery store without a shopping list. Gayle grabbed a cart and headed toward the fresh fruit and vegetables.

We need onions, bell peppers and garlic. I cannot forget to grab some paper towels. Oh yeah, and we need bananas.

She grabbed two yellow onions, a bell pepper and a clove of garlic. Then she turned in the direction of the bananas and there he was.

She looked away quickly.

But her eyes were drawn back to the man across the aisle pondering over the navel oranges.

James Horne looked as handsome as he did the last time she saw him.

She turned around and headed toward a different aisle.

Wow, he still looks good, she thought. I wonder what he is doing in the area. Maybe he is visiting his parents. No, surely they have moved to another duty station by now.

Gayle parked her cart next to the canned goods where she stood for a moment staring into space. She reached in her purse for a tube of lipstick and applied it using the top of a can of Green Giant peas as a makeshift mirror.

I look a mess. And I have gained a few pounds since I last saw him. I cannot let him see me. I need to get out of here.

Gayle left her cart in the middle of the aisle and headed for the front of the store. When she reached the end of the aisle, she looked both ways to make sure there was no sign of James Horne. Just when she thought she was going to make it out safely, she saw him at the front of the store perusing the magazine rack.

He looked up as if on cue and their eyes met.

A massive smile appeared on his face.

"Gayle? I thought that was you. You look beautiful. How are you?"

He took a couple of steps back as if admiring a beautiful piece of art.

"I'm fine, James. How are you? What are you doing in Bossier?" asked Gayle, stumbling over her words.

"I live here now, teaching in Shreveport."

"You're teaching? That is wonderful. I remember how much you wanted to become a teacher."

"And you? I have been keeping up with you in the papers. I read that you went to work for Norman Lear. Are you married?

"Yes, I am. What about you? Did you get married?" she asked, noticing the absence of a ring from his ring finger.

"Me? No, I never married. I stayed in the Air Force long enough to get my degree and then I moved back here. Daddy retired and they bought a house in Shreveport. I bought a house in south Bossier."

An awkward silence stood between them.

"I'd better go," said Gayle.

"It was nice seeing you. Do you think I could call you or something?"

"I don't think that would be a good idea. Maybe we will see each other around. You know how small Shreveport and Bossier can be."

As much as she wanted to catch up on old times, Gayle knew the best thing for her to do was to get out of Brookshire's as quickly as possible.

After all these years, he still looks good. Too bad, I am a married woman.

But if things were different...

CHAPTER 27

Dani

Olivia rubbed her secret blend of spices all over the turkey wings and placed them in the pan of onions and bell peppers. She put the pan in the preheated oven and began cleaning the kitchen. The girls were relieved of their kitchen duty so they could attend a six o'clock youth meeting at the church.

"Is dinner going to be ready before we leave for church?" asked Tasha.

"I don't think so, baby. But I'll wrap up a plate for y'all and put it in the oven."

"It sure smells good. Are you sure it won't be ready?" asked Dani.

"No. I just put the turkey wings in the oven a few minutes ago. Now y'all go in there and change your clothes."

"Man, I hope this is a short meeting. I'm hungry," Dani said as she and Tasha left the kitchen to go change clothes.

Twenty minutes later they sat alone in the church parking lot. "I guess we can roll down the windows and wait for somebody to come and unlock the door," said Dani.

She reached for the plastic knob and cranked the window down. Tasha did the same for her window. The cool evening air brushed against their faces and ushered in the aroma of evening dinner being prepared in the nearby homes.

Tasha's stomach growled.

"I'm going to walk over to the store to get a snack. Do you want something?" she asked.

"You know Olivia said not to leave the church. What if somebody sees you?"

Tasha frowned.

"I'm starving. I will take my chances. We should have grabbed something to eat before we left the house. Anyway, the store is just around the corner. Do you want something or not?"

"OK, I'll buy you some Doritos if you bring me something back."

Nacho Cheese Doritos were Tasha's favorite. Tasha smirked and reached her hand out for the money. Dani grabbed two dollars in quarters from the loose coins in the ashtray.

"I want a bag of Doritos, too, and a Nehi grape soda."

"OK, I'll be right back," Tasha said, opening the door and getting out of the car.

Dani looked around the empty church parking and began to reminisce about the times she walked the empty parking lot with her father. It had been almost seven years since he died, but Dani's memories of her father were clear. She reclined the car seat and closed her eyes.

The crackle of tires rolling over the gravel parking lot snatched her back to reality. She pulled the seat into the upright position and caught sight of Deacon Samuels' dark blue Ford Thunderbird.

He parked, got out of the car and waved to her.

She respectfully returned the wave.

She searched the street for Tasha.

I wish she would hurry back. How long does it take to get a couple of chips and sodas?

Samuels' City of Shreveport maintenance uniform was clean and crisp, as if he was just starting the day. His weighty work boots made a loud clumping noise as he made his way up the front steps to unlock the door. He entered the building. The windows illuminated throughout the edifice as he switched on all the lights.

"No need in waiting out here. Come on in, I won't bite you," yelled Samuels, emerging from the back door and walking toward the Vega.

His cologne reached the car before he did.

"No thank you. I'll wait right here."

"I'm sorry for being late. Traffic was bad. I was supposed to have the door unlocked before any of you got here."

He is acting as if nothing ever happened.

Maybe he did not mean to touch my behind.

Maybe I was over reacting.

"That's OK. I am waiting for Tasha. She'll be right back."

Samuels looked around the parking lot, up and down the street, at the church building and then at Dani.

"If the pastor finds out that I had you waiting out in the car, I'll be in a heap of trouble."

He smiled.

Dani searched the street for Tasha again.

She did not want to cause trouble.

"OK, I'll be in there in a minute."

Deacon Samuels turned around and headed for the back door. Dani searched the street for Tasha one more time, cranked both windows up and grabbed her purse.

She moved as slowly as possible toward the front door of the church.

Something about the situation did not feel right to her.

She did not want to be in the church alone with Samuels, but she did not want to be disrespectful.

Dani decided to wait in the lobby and watch for Tasha through the window.

"Who are you looking for?"

Dani jolted at the sound of Deacon Samuels' voice when he emerged from the men's room on the other side of the lobby.

"Tasha ... she's on her way back. She went to the store," said Dani, her voice trembling.

Samuels smiled.

"I saw her talking to a couple of girls at the store."

He moved closer to Dani.

"You can see everything out of the window ...," he commented, glancing over her head and into the parking lot.

He placed his hands on her shoulders and turned her toward him.

She pulled away.

He pulled her back.

She shrugged her shoulders.

He held tighter.

They stood face to face.

Dani could see the dry and flakey skin on the end of his nose.

The scent of Old Spice cologne burned her nasal passages, and her eyes began to water.

She could hear the hum of the motor from the water fountain.

She prayed silently, *Jesus, please let a car … any car pull into the parking lot.*

"Don't be scared," he said.

His breath reeked of coffee and cigarette smoke.

She tried to pull away again.

The cracked skin from his dry hands caught a strand from her blouse as he rubbed his hands against her shoulder.

He pushed her against the wall and glanced through the window again.

The water fountain's motor clicked off.

He grabbed her face and pulled her closer.

She could hear her heart beating.

Dani clenched her lips between her teeth and turned her head.

She used her hands to push against his chest as hard as she could.

He took a few steps back.

Thank God for the sound of car tires rolling over the graveled parking lot gravel.

"If you tell anyone, I'll deny it. I will say you came on to me. If you know what's good for you, you'll make this our little secret."

He walked away.

Before leaving the lobby, he turned to Dani, winked and said, "Remember, it'll be our little secret."

Dani ran into the ladies' room and waited.

She waited for the lightning.

She waited for the fire and the brimstone.

She just waited.

She waited, and she cried.

She cried, and she waited.

She heard at least two people in the lobby talking about an episode of *Good Times*.

Dani looked at her face in the mirror.

I should have waited in the car for Tasha.

#####

Dani sped out of the parking lot as soon as the meeting was over.

"What took you so long to get back to the church from the store?" Dani yelled at Tasha.

"I ran into some friends. We started talking and I lost track of time."

"Well, you took too long."

"I can take as long as I want to. You cannot tell me what to do. You're not the boss of me!" Tasha shouted.

"If something had happened to you, I would be the one in trouble." Dani took her hand off the steering wheel and pointed at her chest. "So yes, I can tell you what to do."

"Nothing happened to me. I am fine. You got your Doritos and you got your soda. So what's the big deal?"

"Just stay with me next time. OK?"

"OK, what's wrong with you? Did something happen while I was at the store?"

"Nothing's wrong with me. Just don't leave next time, OK."

"OK, don't have a cow. And do not even think about telling on me. Remember, you got something from the store too. If you tell, we'll both be in trouble."

"I said I wouldn't tell, didn't I?"

"Fine."

"Fine."

Tasha turned up the volume on the radio.

The rest of the ride home was silent save the sound of smooth jazz emanating from the car radio.

When the girls entered the house, Tasha checked to see if dinner was in the oven.

"Hey, girls," Olivia said entering the kitchen, dressed in her nightclothes. "Go wash your hands, and I'll warm your food."

"Thanks, Mama."

Olivia stared at Dani for a minute or two.

"What's wrong with you Dani?" she asked.

"Nothing. I'm just tired."

Olivia had an uncanny way of knowing when something was not quite right. She moved closer to Dani and touched her forehead with the back of her hand.

"You don't look well. Wash your hands and eat a little something. Maybe you'll feel better in the morning."

Olivia pulled out two plates of food that had been warming in the oven. She unwrapped the foil covering and place the meals on the table.

"How was the youth meeting?" she asked, joining the girls at the table.

Dani listened as Tasha recapped the meeting.

"It was OK. We're going to have a car wash to raise money, and we're going to have a Christmas play," Tasha said, with her mouth full.

Dani took a bite of her food and pushed the rest of the food around on her plate.

"Were there any adults there?" asked Olivia, stealing a peep at Dani.

"Deacon Samuels was there and of course Sister Collins."

Sister Collins had been the youth director for years. She was the same age as Olivia but way cooler.

"Sister Collins invited everyone to her house for a pizza party after the carwash," said Tasha.

Olivia watched Dani fidgeting with her food. She walked over to the kitchen cabinet, where the Castor oil, Bactine, Bayer baby aspirin, and Father John's cough syrup were stored. She pulled out the baby aspirin, filled a small glass with water, and gave them to Dani.

Dani swallowed the aspirin, pushed her plate aside and went to her room.

CHAPTER 28

Olivia

"Are the girls all right?" asked Leonard when Olivia returned to their bedroom later that night.

"Dani's not feeling well."

"It could be anything. Maybe she ate something that didn't agree with her."

"I doubt it. I think it's more than that."

"What do you mean?"

"I have a feeling it has to do with Samuels."

"Deacon Samuels?"

"Yes."

"Has he done something to make you think he's involved?"

"No, nothing I can put my fingers on. But I have a strange feeling about him. How does the pastor choose which deacon will unlock the doors of the church during the week?"

"One of us usually volunteers. Why?"

"Samuels was at the youth meeting tonight and now Dani suddenly wasn't feeling well when she came home."

"So you think the man did something to Dani because she isn't feeling well? Come on Olivia, be for real."

"Maybe I'm wrong, but will you volunteer to unlock the church doors when the girls have youth meetings?"

"Olivia, you can't accuse a man of wrongdoing because you don't like him."

"I'm not accusing him of anything. Would you do this for me please?"

"Olivia, I'm already at the church almost every day of the week."

"Please," Olivia begged, scooting closer to her husband.

Leonard tried not to smile when she gently kiss him on the ear.

"You say you've got a feeling?" he asked.

"Yes, I've got a feeling."

"I'll do it. I will volunteer to unlock the doors. But now you've got another issue to deal with."

"What's that?"

"You got to deal with me. Now I've got a feeling!"

CHAPTER 29

Gayle

Laverne was disappointed when she saw all the seats occupied on the first row of church. She sashayed back down the aisle delighting in the thought that all eyes were on her.

"Is this seat taken?" she asked Gayle who sat on the end of the fourth row.

"No it's not."

Gayle grabbed her purse and her Bible and moved down one seat. Laverne sat down in her usual short, red dress and red pumps. She smelled like Este Lauder's Youth Dew.

"Hey Gayle, how you been?"

"I'm fine, Laverne. How are you?" whispered Gayle.

"Girl, I almost didn't make it to church ..."

Gayle could tell that Laverne was gearing up for a long story. A few people turned around to see who was talking so loud.

"I can't wait to hear all about it. You'll have to tell me after church," said Gayle, holding her pointer finger to her mouth.

"OK, girl I'll tell you later."

But Laverne found plenty of other things to talk about during church service.

She talked about how pretty the first lady looked in her green two-piece suit and hat.

She talked about how handsome Deacon Samuels was and about what a good dancer he was.

She talked about how hungry she was and that one day she was going to show up at Olivia's for Sunday dinner.

She talked about how sleepy she was until she finally fell asleep just before the pastor gave his sermon.

After the benediction, Gayle gave Laverne a gentle nudge.

"Laverne, church is over. Time to go."

Laverne opened her eyes, picked up her purse and shoes and walked out of the back door.

Gayle found Olivia and the girls in the parking lot.

"Olivia, I'll see you guys at the house."

"OK. You will probably beat us there. If you do, you can start warming up the food."

"Alright."

Gayle turned to see Laverne struggling to get across the graveled parking lot in heels.

"Man, I was trying to get out of here before Laverne caught up with me," said Gayle.

"Just start walking over to your car. Maybe she'll get the message."

"Hey Gayle," yelled Laverne, holding her shoes in one hand and holding her dress down with the other hand.

Gayle looked at Olivia who was taking advantage of the inopportune time to laugh.

"How are you doing, Sister Olivia?"

"I'm fine, Laverne. I was wondering how long it would be before you came out of those shoes."

"There's just no way to be cute and walk across a graveled parking lot in heels. You know what I mean?"

Laverne laughed and released a whiff of her hangover breath.

"Laverne, I know I said we could talk after church, but I really need to get going," said Gayle.

"I gotta go too. I just wanted to find out the skinny on the bad brother you were talking to at Brookshire's the other day."

Gayle felt like she was the woman in the Bible caught in the act of adultery. Laverne stood waiting for an answer.

Olivia pretended not to eavesdrop.

"The other day … uh … that was James Horne. He's a friend of mine from high school."

Gayle glanced at Olivia who was standing with her mouth wide open.

"He sure was fine. Is he married?"

"No, he's not married," said Gayle.

"What about a girlfriend …anybody serious?"

"I'm not sure. Listen Laverne, I gotta go. We'll talk later, OK?"

"That's cool. Maybe I'll say something to him the next time he comes into the store."

"That's a good idea. You should do that. I'll talk to you later, gotta go."

Gayle hurried to her car. She started the engine and backed out of the parking lot avoiding eye contact with Olivia.

CHAPTER 30

Olivia

"Gayle…Gayle, honey wake up," said Olivia.

In the recesses of her mind, Gayle could hear someone calling her name as she slept on the couch in Olivia's living room.

Gayle opened her eyes to find Olivia sitting on the other end of the couch.

"Where's is everybody?" she asked.

"Dani's in her room on the phone. Leonard and Tasha went to take Sister Davis a plate of food. It is just you and me. I cut a piece of cake for you. Would you like a cup of coffee to go with it?"

Gayle noticed two small plates sitting on the coffee table each holding a fork and a healthy slice of pound cake.

I feel a lecture coming. Olivia is going to try to get me to talk about William and I know she is going to ask about James.

"I'll take a cup of coffee, thank you."

Gayle folded the blanket while Olivia made two cups of coffee.

"How long was I asleep?"

"Long enough to clear the room with your snoring."

"Really? Was I that loud?"

"It's OK. We just kept turning the volume up on the TV."

Olivia brought the two cups of coffee into the living room and sat them on the coffee table. She sat on the opposite end of the couch facing Gayle.

Gayle took a bite of the pound cake.

"I don't know how you do it Olivia. This cake is delicious."

"Mama taught me how to make this cake when you were a baby. It was daddy's favorite."

"I remember how good mama could cook. Remember her homemade biscuits?"

"I sure do. Mama was a good cook."

A bit of sadness came over the room as they took a mental journey back to an earlier time and place.

"Can I have the recipe?" asked Gayle washing away the wistful lump in her throat with a sip of hot coffee.

"Of course you can. Maybe you can make it and bring some over the next time you and William come by."

Great segue.

"I can do that."

"How is William by the way? We don't see much of him."

"Besides being bummed out about not finding a job, he's fine."

"Are the two of you getting along any better?"

"I guess so," said Gayle taking another bite of cake.

Olivia sensed Gayle's hesitancy.

"I just remembered that you were cutting back on sweets. I shouldn't have put that cake in front of you."

"It's OK. Once I saw it, I forgot all about my diet. I know I'll have to pay for it either with a few more pounds or a few more jazzercise classes."

"I saw you looking at that cake earlier but you passed on a slice after dinner. What made you change your mind?"

"Honestly I didn't think about it until you put it in front of me. I remembered how much I enjoyed your pound cake. It's always so moist and it melts in my mouth."

Olivia smiled.

"I'm glad you enjoyed it. It is funny how things that look good can be tempting. It could be something we weren't even thinking about and out of nowhere the devil tries to tempt us into sin."

She is not talking about cake anymore.

"Olivia, I'm not going to do anything I'll regret later," said Gayle with a tone of anger.

"I'm not accusing you of anything. I just want you to be aware of the tricks of the devil."

"I'll remember that. I should probably get going now."

"OK, I made a plate of food for you to take to William."

"Thanks Olivia. I know he'll appreciate it."

Olivia headed towards the kitchen.

Gayle thought about her husband. Then she thought of James and the fun times they once had together. She thought about how he made her feel beautiful, smart, and special.

She left her plate in the kitchen with Olivia singing, "Yield not to Temptation".

CHAPTER 31

Dani

The bell rang and students rushed to their lockers and then to their designated buses or cars. Most of them wore that *end of the day* look with hairs out of place, lunch-stained clothes and girls with little signs of the makeup that covered their faces earlier that day.

A string of yellow buses lined the school's driveway. The empty buses sat with doors opened waiting to greet weary learners. Some bus drivers sat behind their steering wheel enjoying the quiet before the storm, and others chatted among themselves along the driveway.

A few students remained for after-school activities. Dani was almost at her car when a blue Ford Thunderbird parked across the street caught her attention.

Is that Deacon Samuels' car?

"Hey, Dani let's go," Tasha yelled.

An irritated Tasha leaned against the Vega with her legs crossed, her hands on her hips, and her eyes rolling.

Any other time Dani would have tarried her steps in an attempt to further antagonize Tasha. But today she wanted to find out who was sitting in the blue Ford Thunderbird across the street from the school.

"What took you so long?"

Dani ignored Tasha's question, unlocked the driver's side door and got in the car. She reached over to unlock Tasha's door.

"I know you hear me. What took so long? How would you like it if I kept you waiting out here in the hot sun?"

"Okay, I'm sorry. Get in the car so we can go."

Tasha got in the car.

They cranked the windows down to release some of the smoldering heat from inside of the car.

Dani merged her bright orange Vega between April Watson's shiny new baby blue Trans-am and Archie Exford's Dodge pick-up.

When Dani reached the corner, she could see that it was definitely Deacon Samuels sitting behind the wheel of the blue Thunderbird with a repulsive sneer on his face.

Dani turned the corner quickly.

"Slow down. Are you trying to kill us?"

"Sorry, it's just that I'm in a rush to get home."

"What's the hurry?"

"Nothing. I'm slowing down."

Dani put her foot on the brake and slowed the car.

She checked the rearview mirror.

There was no sign of Samuels.

They traveled the rest of the way home in silence.

I do not have a choice. Now I have to tell Olivia because this is a crazy man.

Dani parked the car in front of the house and headed for the kitchen phone.

She began to chew the inside of her bottom lip. The warm salty fluid oozed against her tongue.

Gayle! I will call Gayle.

Dani picked up the phone and began dialing Gayle's number.

If I tell Gayle, she will worry so much that she will eventually tell Olivia.

I cannot tell Aretha. She would not tell anybody but she would tease me about being scared.

"Do you want some of this banana pudding?" asked Tasha.

Dani hung up the phone and watched as Tasha pulled the Tupperware dish from the refrigerator.

"The cookies are soft now that they've been in the refrigerator for a while. Do you want me to grab a bowl for you?"

"No thanks. I am going to start my chores and do some homework. I have a math test tomorrow."

"Good. Then I can eat all of this by myself. There's only a little bit left."

Tasha smiled and placed a spoonful of banana pudding in her mouth.

Dani went to her room.

"Somebody keeps calling and hanging up," said Tasha, entering the room with a scowl on her face. "If the phone rings again, will you answer it?"

"If they won't talk to you, what makes you think they'll talk to me?"

"Will you pick it up anyway, please?"

"Okay, I guess so."

Tasha walked out and closed the door behind her.

The phone rang again.

Dani picked up the receiver.

"Hello?"

There was a slight pause, but Dani could hear someone breathing on the other end of the phone.

"You looked nice today. I don't get to see you dressed in jeans when you are at church," said the caller.

Dani hung up the phone as soon as she recognized Deacon Samuels' voice.

CHAPTER 32

Gayle

Gayle listened to William complain about the lack of available jobs the next morning. When she could not bear another moment, she headed for the public library. She sat in a secluded reading area inside the public library grueling through pages of research on peer pressure for an idea she had for a play.

"Is this seat taken?" asked James, standing in front of Gayle. He was dressed in a pair of jeans and a white button-down shirt.

"Hi James, sure have a seat. I was just about to leave."

"Do you have to rush off? I was hoping that we could chat a while. I see you still like to spend time in the library?"

"I sure do. But I could say the same thing about you."

"I'm trying to find innovative ways to stimulate the minds of my students."

James sat with his elbows resting on the table. He began to rub his thumb against his pointer finger. Gayle could sense that he wanted to say something.

"Look Gayle, I just want to say that I'm sorry," he said, touching her hand.

Gayle pulled her hand away.

"What are you apologizing for?"

"For not writing you back all those years ago. I should have stayed in contact. But it was so hard for me."

"That was a long time ago. Things happen for a reason."

"But I want you to know that it was hard for me to be so far away from you. I just could not bear the thought of not being with you. I knew that one of those college boys would try to make a move on you."

Gayle thought about the many nights she longed to hear James say those very words. She remembered how he tried to pressure her to move to California but he did not want to get married right away.

"We were both pretty stubborn back then."

"Yes, we were. You were determined to be a writer and I was determined to be an Airman. If I had it to do all over again …"

This is the part where I am supposed to tell him that I am happily married.

But those were not words that came from her mouth.

Gayle thought she could hear Olivia's voice saying, "It's funny how we can be tempted by things that look so good."

"But we don't have it to do all over again, do we?" asked Gayle as she assembled her things.

"Can I at least walk you to your car?"

"I don't think that's such a good idea."

"What if I promise not to talk about the past or what might have been or anything like that? In fact, I will keep quiet while you tell me about your next project."

Before Gayle could answer yea or nay, James gathered both their books in his arms.

She stood and together they walked toward the door. He held the door open for her as they walked out of the library.

It was a quiet evening with an occasional car driving down Barksdale Boulevard. The sweet smell of Southern Maid Donuts drifted from across the street.

"So what project are you working on now?" asked James glancing at Gayle with a smile.

She tried not to look into his eyes.

"I'm working on a play that I hope to stage at the municipal auditorium."

"What's it about?"

"It's about teens and peer pressure. The cast will be mostly teens. I hope to send a message that it is not cool to do drugs and things like that. And of course I hope to introduce as many of them as possible to Jesus."

"You know just last week I found a bag of pot under one of the desk in my classroom. It fell out of a student's pocket when he got up from his desk. I watched as another student picked it up and stashed it for him."

"How did you handle that?"

"I wasn't sure what it was at first. I mean I know what a bag of weed looks like, but I did not think that these particular students would have something like that. Anyway, I talked with both of them and of course we had to take it to the principal."

"When I think about all the things that Dani and Tasha have to deal with now days, it makes me want to do something. You know Olivia keeps a tight rein but a lot of kids don't have that kind of support at home."

"Have you thought about bringing some of the churches in on your project?"

"I've thought about that. Of course Gates of Heaven will be involved, but I've also been talking to several of the other pastors in town."

"Don't forget about the Base Chapel. I know we're not Baptist or anything but we'd love to be involved."

"You're still going to the chapel even though your dad has retired."

"I sure am. I am a deacon now. You should come and visit sometime. Of course I mean you and your husband."

It would be easier to get Olivia to visit a church that was not Baptist than it would be to get my William inside a church of any denomination.

"Thanks for the invitation, maybe we'll take you up on it someday," said Gayle as she unlocked her car door and sat in the driver's side.

Just then, a car drove by blowing its horn. James and Gayle caught sight of the burgundy Cutlass Supreme driving by with an arm waving out of the driver's window.

"That's probably one of my students," said James.

"I'd better get going," said Gayle shutting the door and starting the engine.

"It was nice to see you again, Gayle," said James as Gayle barreled out of the parking lot and onto Barksdale Boulevard. She waved goodbye and James' image faded in the rearview mirror.

I am afraid that was not one of your students, Mr. Horne.

That was Olivia doing a Holy Ghost drive-by.

CHAPTER 33

Gayle

Gayle opened the front door to find William standing in the living room looking like a child caught with his hand in the cookie jar.

"Gayle, I didn't expect you back so soon," he said holding two large takeout boxes from China King restaurant.

A bouquet of bright-red roses sat in the center of the coffee table.

"What's the occasion?" asked Gayle.

The Commodores played on the radio in the background.

"I wanted to surprise you."

"And you did."

"Do you remember Big G from New York?"

"Yeah"

"He's got this gig and he needs my help."

"What do you mean he needs your help?"

She dropped her things on the sofa and crossed her arms in front of her.

"He's offering me a chance to make it big. He has a gig working on a new show. They need dancers and he can almost guarantee me a spot."

William crossed his finger and held them in the air.

Gayle stared at her husband. She could not remember the last time she had seen him so excited.

"What are you saying?"

"I'm saying that I tried it your way."

"So you're leaving, just like that?"

"I'd ask you to go, but you have your family here and you are working on a couple of projects.

"William, do you even know what things I'm working on?"

"What difference does it make? You seem to be doing alright."

There was a hint of resentment in his voice. She looked at the roses and the take-out dinner.

Her eyes burned with fury.

She thought about asking him to reconsider but the more she thought about it, the better his plans sounded to her.

With all the enthusiasm she could muster, Gayle looked at her husband and said, "Let me help you pack."

CHAPTER 34

Gayle

Gayle agonized over how and when to tell the family that her husband was gone. But a few days after William left, she decided to break the news to Olivia.

Gayle stood immobilized at the foot of the bed feeling as if she was in the principal's office. Gayle knew she had contributed to the breakup of her marriage and she did not know if it was too late for reconciliation.

"Gayle, what's wrong?"

"It's William …"

"What about William?"

Now she is being sarcastic. That is why I do not like to talk to her about my business.

"He's gone."

"He's gone where?"

"He's gone to New York."

"When will he be back?"

"I'm not sure. He got a job."

"That's good news, isn't it? Are you going to join him?"

"No. We thought it would be a good idea to have some time apart."

"What do you mean?"

"We have issues we need to resolve?"

"What kind of issues?"

"First of all he doesn't go to church. And he drinks too much."

"I see. He probably went to church before you two got married. He was suckering you in and made you think he was a regular churchgoer. Besides that, he probably did not drink alcohol before you married him. And I am sure he never saw you take a drink. He tricked you into thinking that you were marrying a man who did not drink alcohol. I can't wait to give him a piece of my mind."

Gayle rolled her eyes.

"OK, I knew he drank before I married him and I even shared a few drinks with him. But he doesn't know when to stop," Gayle grumbled.

"Oh, I see."

"He drinks all day and he doesn't want to work."

"Did he have a job when you met him?"

"That's how we met. I hired him for one of my plays."

"I mean before that. Where did he work?"

"I don't know. We got married so quickly. We didn't have enough time to learn much about each ..."

Gayle refused to give Olivia the pleasure of hearing the end of that sentence.

"We just have to work a few things out, that's all."

"And you can do that living thousands of miles apart?"

"I'm not sure. I don't even know if he really has a job."

"Have a seat," said Olivia, "and tell me everything from the beginning."

CHAPTER 35

Olivia

Gayle immersed herself into her writing to keep her mind off the state of her marriage. It had been almost two weeks since William left. Olivia sat in her bedroom talking to the girls. Olivia and Gayle sat in the king-sized bed with their backs against the headboard. Tasha laid side-ways across the foot of the bed and Dani sat in the upholstered chair.

"I need to hire two stage managers to help me with my stage play. Would y'all be interested in helping me?" asked Gayle.

"What do you need us to do?" asked Dani.

"I need one of you to be responsible for checking in the actors during the auditions. And I need the other one of you to announce the actors as they enter the stage to audition. I will probably need someone to run the stopwatch for me. The actors will get two minutes to audition. I will pay you guys if you help me."

"It's a deal," said Dani.

"Yeah," said Tasha.

"Is that alright with you Olivia?" asked Gayle.

"It is fine with me as long as it doesn't interfere with homework."

"The auditions are Saturday. I will pick them up around eight in the morning and take them to breakfast. There won't be enough time for them to help clean the house before they leave, though."

Gayle gave the girls a wink.

"That's fine, but I'll make breakfast. No need to spend money if you don't have to."

"Some of the kids were talking about the play after church today. Shirley Faye said she was auditioning," said Tasha.

"So did Lori and Denita."

"That's great. I have had so many positive responses. Deacon Samuels came up to me after church and asked if he could help."

"Samuels?" ask Olivia.

"Yeah. Why? What's wrong?"

"I'm not comfortable with him being around the girls. There's something about him that doesn't sit right with me."

The girls turned their focus to the television and respectfully pretended not to listen to the grown-folks conversation.

"As much as I hate to admit it, your feelings are usually right on the money. I will ask him to help with advertising or something like that. He will not have a reason to be at the rehearsals."

"Okay, but I want you to watch him Gayle. You do not want him around any of those young girls. It's like asking for trouble."

"I'll keep that in mind."

CHAPTER 36

Dani

On Saturday morning Gayle stood on the stage next to a six-foot long folding table giving instructions.

"Loretta, you and I will sit at this table so we can talk privately during the auditions."

Loretta was one of the meanest black women Dani ever had the pleasure of meeting. The six-foot-seven inch bald-headed woman carried most of her two-hundred-sixty pounds in her midsection.

"You don't expect me to sit in that do you?" said Loretta pointing at one of the three folding chairs positioned behind the table.

"I'll see if I can find something more comfortable. Tasha, would you put the signs on the outside of the entrance and in the hallway to point the way to this room?"

"Sure."

"The signs and the tape are on the end of the table. Thank, you sweetie."

Tasha grabbed the signs and ambled toward the hallway.

"Dani, I'm going to need your help with audition forms. Would you distribute and collect an audition form from everyone?"

"Sure, where are the forms?"

"They're in the trunk of my car. Would you mind getting them for me?"

"Sure."

"Here are my keys and don't drive off little girl."

Gayle reached in her purse and groped for the keys. She tossed them to Dani.

"What about my chair? I need something to sit on," grumbled Loretta.

Dani went to the car to find the audition forms and Gayle went to the front office to ask the manager for another chair.

The parking lot was empty except for Gayle's car and two city vehicles. Dani assumed the city vehicles belonged to the auditorium employees. She unlocked the trunk of the car.

A blue Ford Thunderbird entered the parking lot and pulled into the parking spot next to Gayle's car.

"Let me get that for you," yelled Samuels.

"No thanks. I got it."

She held the box against her chest and began a sprint toward the front door.

"Watch out for that …"

Before he could complete the sentence, Dani and the audition forms were laying in the middle of the parking lot.

"Are you OK?

"I'm fine."

"Let me help you up."

"I can get up by myself. I'm not hurt."

Her new Jordace jeans ripped at the knee.

"Aw …that's nothing that a little TLC won't cure," Samuels said rubbing his hand over her knee.

Despite the pain, she stood quickly. That is when she saw the pothole.

"Why don't you leave me alone? What are you doing here anyway?"

"Didn't your sister tell you? I'm helping out with the play."

Dani remembered the conversation between Gayle and Olivia. She doubted seriously that Gayle knew he was coming.

"Look, if you don't leave me alone, I'm going to tell Olivia."

"If you were going to do that, you would have done it a long time ago. No, I think you'll keep our little secret."

"Are you all right ma'am?"

An old white man with a pleasant grandpa face stood at the entrance to the building. He wore khaki pants and a polo shirt.

"I was watching from my window and I saw you fall," said grandpa.

Grandpa picked up the box. Samuels grabbed the loose documents and placed them in the box.

"I'm fine."

"Let's go inside, I'll get a bandage for you," said grandpa.

Grandpa held the door open for Dani and gave Samuels a suspicious look.

Gayle and Loretta stopped what they were doing when Dani hobbled in with the two men in tow.

"There was a little accident," said grandpa.

"What happened?" asked Gayle.

"I tripped, that's all. I'm OK."

"There is a pothole out there. It was covered with a traffic cone. I'll place another traffic cone out there and weigh it down with something so no one else gets hurt."

"That should have been taken care of before we got here," said Loretta, rolling her eyes at grandpa.

"Are you OK Dani?" asked Gayle.

"Yeah. I'm just going to clean it up in the bathroom."

"I'll get the first-aid kit," said Grandpa.

The girls headed for the bathroom and the grandpa went to find the first aid kit.

"Is there something I can do for you Deacon Samuels?" asked Gayle.

"I thought I'd drop by to see if you needed any help?"

"No. But thank you. And by the way, I appreciate all you've done to get us some radio airtime."

"No problem."

"I'd invite you to stay but these are closed auditions."

"I understand. No problem."

Samuels turned to leave.

"Thanks again."

Loretta looked at Gayle.

"Since when were the auditions closed?"

"Since just now."

CHAPTER 37

Gayle

Later that night Loretta sat at Gayle's kitchen table wearing a two-toned green muumuu and a pair of men's white crew socks.

She bathed a piece of Popeye's chicken in Louisiana hot sauce and popped it in her mouth.

"I bought an advertising spot in the entertainment section of the paper," said Gayle.

"That reminds me, I need to call the station tomorrow morning and ask about free tickets as prizes for their listeners," said Loretta wiping her hands on a paper towel.

"I wish we could find a part for everyone that auditioned."

"What do you have to drink?"

"There's Diet Coke and bottled water in the fridge. What would you like?"

"I'll take a couple of bottles of water, thanks."

Gayle walked over to the refrigerator and grabbed two bottles of water.

"What's up with the dude you kicked out of the auditions?"

"Which dude?"

"The one that got us the contact and the great deal with the radio station."

"Samuels?"

Gayle placed the bottle water on the table in front of Loretta and returned to the refrigerator for a bottle of Diet Coke.

"Yeah, that's the one. What's the deal with him anyway?"

"Olivia doesn't like him for some reason. I promised to keep him away from the girls."

Gayle removed an ice tray from the freezer and two glasses from the cupboard. She broke the ice apart and placed a few cubes in each glass.

"I don't blame her. I did not like the way he looked at Dani. Dani didn't seem to like him too much either."

Gayle placed one glass on the table in front of Loretta, popped open her can of Diet Coke and poured it into the other glass.

"And who was that guy that dropped the first group of kids off?"

"That was James."

"James?"

"James Horne."

Loretta dropped what she was doing and looked at Gayle.

"You mean the first man you ever loved James?" she asked.

Gayle rattled the ice cubes and took a swallow of her Diet Coke.

"You know entirely too much about me."

"That may be true. But you have got a lot of explaining to do. I come up here to help you with this play and I find out you are separated from your husband."

"I'm not separated from my husband; we're just not living together right now."

"OK. Then I find out that you have reconnected with your old boyfriend -your first love. So what's the story?" asked Loretta swallowing a half bottle of water.

"What do you mean?"

"What's going on with you and James?"

"Nothing"

Gayle grabbed a chicken wing from the box. She separated the drummette and mid-joint.

"If you could do it, and no one would find out, would you do it?"

"Do what?"

Loretta rolled her eyes.

The phone rang.

Gayle picked up the receiver.

"Hello? … Hey, can you hold on a second?" she said.

"I'm going to take this call in my room," she said to Loretta. "Would you hang up when I pick up the other extension?"

"Sure. But don't think that I didn't notice."

"Notice what?"

"That you didn't answer my question."

Gayle smiled and walked to her room.

"I got it," she yelled to Loretta.

Loretta placed the phone onto the receiver and continued to review production notes.

"How are you William?" asked Gayle.

"I'm fine, Babe. It is good to hear your voice. How are you?"

"I'm good."

Deep down Gayle wanted to hear him say things were not working out.

"I'm working the lights on a Broadway show. It could turn into something permanent."

"What happened to the dancing gig?"

"It didn't pan out, but Big G was able to get this job for me."

"That's great William. I'm happy for you."

"How's your project going?"

"What project William? What project am I working on?"

"Look Gayle, I'm trying here. Can you cut me some slack?"

Gayle thought about what her husband said. He was trying.

"I'm staging a play. The cast is made entirely of teenagers. And I am still working on my screenplay. It should be done soon."

"That's awesome Gayle. Are Tasha and Dani in the play?"

"They are working as stage managers. So where are you staying? Do you have an apartment?"

"Big G is letting me sleep on his couch in exchange for helping out with groceries and stuff. And he makes me go to church with him on Sundays."

"What?"

"I thought that would get your attention. He is making me go to church in exchange for sleeping on his couch. It is not that bad. He goes to this small church down the street and he sings in the choir."

"Big G?"

"Yeah, Big G. I figure if he can get something out of going to church, maybe I can too."

CHAPTER 38

Dani

After a few months of rehearsal, the characters in *Pump up the Praise* were ready to step off the pages and onto the stage. The play was scheduled to run Friday, Saturday and Sunday nights for two consecutive weekends in July.

Dani, Tasha, Aretha and a few other girls from Gates of Heaven served as greeters.

Dani wore a black polyester skirt and a white blouse with a laced collar. The full skirt brought little attention to her ever-growing curves. Tasha wore a black A-line skirt and a white button-down blouse. Both girls wore white-canvas shoes.

"Let's look around a little before the play starts," said Tasha.

"Yeah, let's go downstairs."

"That's a good idea. The bathrooms are downstairs, let's take a look," said Dani.

The girls walked downstairs.

At the end of the stairway was a long hallway with three walls decorated in a Mardi gras theme. Each wall contained a door. The men's room sat on the left, and the ladies' room sat on the right. An unmarked door stood straight ahead. A large flowerpot with a small tree decorated with branches and Mardi gras masks stood next to each bathroom door.

A rich-plum colored carpet covered the floor and continued throughout the entrance of the sitting area in the ladies' room where a large gold-trimmed mirror covered one wall. Strings of purple and green beads hung from the mirror. Green washcloths rolled up like Tootsie Rolls were place next to each of the three sinks below the mirror.

"This is a nice bathroom," said Dani looking around the room, "they even have purple, green and gold soap."

The girls explored the rest of the bathroom and wandered in the hallway admiring the five-foot Mardi Gras Float wall covering, the colorful tragedy/comedy masks and other commemorative decorations.

"I wonder what's in there?" asked Tasha, pointing to the door at the end of the hall.

"There's only one way to find out."

Dani opened the door to an unadorned eight by ten inch closet. Metal bookshelves containing boxes, cleaning supplies and discarded Mardi gras decorations lined the walls. A glass-globe covered a light bulb hanging from ceiling light. The room was damp and moldy.

"It's just a closet. Look at the old boxes and stuff," said Tasha.

"That looks like some of the programs for the play," said Dani pointing to a box next to the door.

"Those are for the rest of the performances. I heard Aunt Gayle ask Deacon Samuels to put them in the closet for her."

"Deacon Samuels is here?" Dani asked.

"Yes, he was helping the men move things around back stage. Do you want to go look around back there?"

"No, we already did that during rehearsals. Let's go back to the lobby with everybody else."

If Samuels is here, I want to be around by as many people as possible. He would not dare try anything around a crowd of people.

CHAPTER 39

Olivia

Olivia's face oozed with pride for her little sister. She flounced down the aisle in a purple-layered dress, purple and gold twister-bead necklace, gold-elastic belt and matching purple pumps. It took some coercing on Gayle's part to get Olivia to leave the matching purple hat at home.

Leonard strutted in like a proud papa looking dapper in his blue pinstriped suit and lavender knit square-bottomed tie.

Gayle had instructed the ushers to provide nothing less than VIP treatment for Leonard and Olivia. They were to be ushered to the front row prior to the start of the play and ushered back stage after the play.

Theatergoers were welcomed with a smile and a program when they entered the spacious lobby.

Dani thought she recognized a familiar face in the crowd.

The afro was gone and so were about ten pounds, but the man standing in the doorway holding a dozen long-stemmed red roses was her brother-in-law, William.

"Dani is that you?" he asked.

"It's me. Hey William. Does Gayle know you're here?"

Dani wanted to hug him but thought better of it.

He instinctively wrapped his arms around her neck and gave her a kiss on the cheek.

"Hey Uncle William," said Tasha, recognizing his presence.

William hugged and kissed his niece.

"No, she doesn't know I'm here," he said returning to his conversation with Dani.

"She's back stage. Do you want me to take you back there?"

"No thanks. I will find my way. But would you keep these roses in a safe place for me?" asked William, handing her the bouquet.

Dani brought them to her nose and inhaled.

"These are nice. I'll give them to Olivia."

"Maybe you shouldn't give them to Olivia. Is there any place you can keep them safe for me? I'd like to give them to Gayle after the play."

Dani and Tasha thought about William's request for a minute.

"There's a closet by the bathroom downstairs," said Dani.

Tasha nodded in support of Dani's suggestion.

"Would you mind putting them in there until after the curtain call?"

"Sure."

Man, while I am putting these flowers in the closet, Tasha will get to tell Olivia about William.

"Thanks," said William as he hurried backstage.

Dani left to put the roses in the closet.

And Tasha left to share the news with Olivia.

CHAPTER 40

Gayle

William stood in a corner backstage admiring his wife. He had missed her over these last months. Sure, he enjoyed the long phone conversations and the letters but it did not compare to seeing her with his own eyes.

She was as beautiful as the day they met.

She appeared to be happy.

She was after all in her own element.

She stood alone behind a podium with her head bowed.

Others may have assumed she was reading over the script or perhaps making last minute revisions.

But he knew she was praying.

Organized chaos raged around him, but all he could see was his five-foot four-inch Nubian princess bride.

Intuitively, Gayle raised her head and looked at William.

They gazed into each other's eyes for a moment.

An anxious pause ensued.

The corners of Gayle's lips began curling upward.

She could not find her words.

He walked over to her and in that familiar baritone voice he said, "I didn't want to miss your opening night."

CHAPTER 41

Olivia

On the first row of the theater Olivia and Leonard were being informed that William was back in town and that he was surprising Gayle at that very moment.

An anxious Olivia rose from her seat.

Leonard reached for Olivia's elbow and slid his hand down her arm until her hand lay in his. He gently pulled her back down into her seat.

"I just want to check on her, that's all," she said.

"She'll be fine. This is between a man and his wife."

Olivia reluctantly settled in her seat.

"Then you'd better start praying."

"Olivia, Gayle will be fine. She is a grown woman. She knows where to find you if she needs you."

"I mean you better start praying for William. Because if he hurts my sister I'm going to break both of his legs and stick one of those Mardi Gras mask …"

Suddenly the theater lights dimmed and Loretta appeared on stage in spotlight announcing, "Ladies and Gentlemen, welcome to One Righteous Theatre's production of *Pump up the Praise* by Gayle Ferguson."

CHAPTER 42

Dani

Pump up the Praise opened with the main character walking across the stage having fun with her friends. The actors began to relax into character and delivered one delicious line after another.

The greeters remained in the lobby during Act I. Tasha and Aretha stood near the front door gossiping about the array of teenage boys in the theater that night. Dani put her ear to the door and listened as the main character got into a fight with her friends over a bag of marijuana.

"Did you see Beryl from Bossier High?" asked Tasha with a smile.

"Yeah, I saw him. I gave him a program," said Aretha.

"Did he say anything to you?"

"No, he's with that cheerleader."

"She's so pretty. What was she wearing?"

"She had on a plaid jumpsuit. I think she looks like Sue Ellen on *Dallas*."

Dani pulled her ear away from the door and searched the lobby for Samuels. She was certain he was lurking nearby and she could not shake the feeling that someone was watching her.

Tasha, Aretha and a few of the other greeters sang and danced along with the cast during the musical numbers. As the drama unfolded, the main character graduated to harder drugs.

Soon the main character was hanging on for dear life.

It was time for intermission.

CHAPTER 43

Dani

Act II opened with the main character lying in a hospital surrounded by friends and loved ones.

As the play developed, the main character began the painful journey to give up drugs.

There was more singing and more dancing.

As the conclusion neared, the main character suffered through the stages of drug withdrawal. The uncompromising message conveyed by the cast of teenagers was that drug use is a direct road to death.

"It's almost over. I am going to the bathroom before the final scene. You want to go with me?" asked Dani.

"No thanks, I went right after intermission," said Tasha.

"Me too," said Aretha.

"I'll be right back, then. I gotta go," said Dani, and she hurried out of the door, through the hallway and down the stairs.

When she finished up in the bathroom, Dani washed her hands and took a quick look in the mirror.

My hair is a mess, she thought. I wish I had a comb with me. She ran her fingers through her hair, ran out of the bathroom and into Samuels.

He grabbed her arm, placed his hands over her mouth and pulled her into the storage closet.

Samuels held her back against his front and pressed his hand so hard against her mouth that she thought her teeth would crack.

It was dark.

The room smelled like cleaning supplies, musk and roses.

She tried to remember the placement of metal bookshelves and the boxes.

She reached around for something to grab, anything to use as a weapon.

He laughed.

She cried.

He groped.

She cried.

He laughed again.

She bent her knee and raised her right foot high. Then she bent her other leg slightly at the knee to provide support. She aimed her heel and hips in a straight line and back kicked Samuels right between his legs.

Dani ran out of the closet, up the stairs, through the lobby and into the theater where the frenzied crowd was offering a standing ovation.

CHAPTER 44

Olivia

Olivia scanned the audience during the standing ovation. She saw James Horne sitting on the left side two rows from the back with a handful of long-stemmed red roses. Almost instantly an usher appeared next to Olivia and Leonard, "I'm here to escort you back stage," he said.

"Leonard, why don't you go ahead? I'll meet you back there in a few minutes?"

"Yes, I see someone I haven't seen in a while. I want to say hello."

"You want me to wait?"

"No, Gayle will be looking for us. Tell her that I'll be there in a minute."

Olivia meandered her way through the crowd. When she reached James, Olivia extended her hand.

"James, it's nice to see you."

James held the roses in one hand and extended the other toward Olivia.

"Thank you, ma'am. It is good to see you as well. Wow, the performance was wonderful. You must be very proud?"

James swallowed.

"I sure am?"

"You look beautiful as always. You have not changed a bit. Is Mr. Howard here?"

"Yes. He went to find William and Gayle. Have you met Gayle's husband, William?"

"William? No, I have not met him. Is he here?" James asked, trying very hard to hide his disappointment.

"Yes. I can introduce you to him if you like."

James suddenly became aware of the roses in his hand and he wanted to crawl under one of the theatre seats.

"I'd love to meet him, but I brought some people with me and they're anxious to get home."

"Are you sure? It'll only take a second."

"Yes, ma'am I'm sure. But thank you so much. Would you let Gayle know that I enjoyed the play?"

"I sure will. Goodnight."

CHAPTER 45

Gayle

Gayle and William stayed up until midnight sharing a pizza and enjoying each other's company. They sat on the couch listening to a Michael Jackson's *Off the Wall* album.

"We still have a lot to talk about," said Gayle.

"I know," said William, picking a pepperoni off the pizza and throwing it in his mouth.

Gayle giggled.

"I'm so sorry for hurting you," he said, "All I wanted was to take care of you and I couldn't do that before. I went about it the wrong way, which made the situation worse."

She took a swallow of her diet soda and watched him.

I hope he is telling the truth, but what if he starts acting crazy again.

"I forgive you William, but we still have a lot of work to do."

"I know we do. I hear you and I want to find a way to move past this. I understand you might not be ready to welcome me back. Let us take it slow. I have to be back at work tomorrow but I'll keep coming back here until you are ready to move back to New York with me."

"I don't know what to say,"

"Just say that you'll think about it."

Gayle hesitated; she did not want to lie.

"The only thing that I can promise is that I forgive you. It is going to take some time to trust you. God is going to have to help me with that."

"About God ..."

"Yes, about God."

William placed his index finger on Gayle's lips.

"What I was going to say was that I believe in God."

Gayle moved his finger away from her mouth.

"Look William, don't play with me. Are you serious?"

"I always thought of God like I did Santa Clause or the Easter Bunny. I thought He was something people believed in because of stories that had no merit. Then Big G insisted that I go to church with him. I had no choice really. I needed a place to stay. I eventually started reading the Bible."

William noticed the stunned look on Gaye's face.

"You see Big G didn't just go to church, he went to Sunday school before church. Because I did not have a car, I had to tag along for Sunday school. Anyway, in class, we read and discussed the Scriptures. It began to make sense to me. I mean there is a lot that I do not understand. But I know that there is a God and guess what?"

"What?"

"I believe in His son, Jesus."

Gayle began to cry.

"I know, it's truly a miracle," said William, placing his arms around Gayle.

"I don't want to mislead you. I am a work in progress. I mean I still like a Budweiser now and then ..."

Gayle plugged his mouth with a big kiss.

"You know I even apologized to Leonard and Olivia," he said after breathing a sigh of relief.

"You did?"

"She wasn't very happy to see me at first. I thought she was going to slap me."

Gayle laughed.

"I'm not surprised."

"But she came around after I made my intentions known to them."

"And what are your intentions?"

"I intend to make you fall in love with me all over again. I want you to want to be with me. You make me want to be a better man."

Gayle tried to catch her breath.

"What did Olivia have to say?"

"Not much. But she did ask me if I'd like for Loretta to spend the night at her house?"

"Are you sure that you understood her correctly?"

"Yes, I am. Loretta's not here is she?"

Gayle smiled.

"How's your screenplay coming along?" asked William.

"My screenplay? You remember my screenplay?"

"Yes, I do. Of course, I remember. You were going to write a movie that would spread the Gospel to young people like never before. You wanted to take back the big screen for Jesus. You said, 'I'm tired of the big screen being used to steal, kill and destroy our young people,'" said William in a voice mimicking his wife.

Gayle was touched that William remembered.

"So where are you in the process?"

"I finished the screenplay."

"Wow. How long did it take you?"

"I started working on it before we met. So it's been a long time."

"You don't know how proud I am of you. That is an amazing accomplishment. So what's the next step?"

"I've researched a number of film production companies that might be interested in my script and now I need to submit query letters. I'll get started on that after the play closes."

"Why wait. Let's start addressing envelopes tonight."

"Tonight? William you have a plane to catch tomorrow and I have over two hundred names."

"Gayle, please let me help you with this."

"Are you sure?"

"It's the least I can do. You get the envelopes and I'll start a pot of coffee."

William and Gayle devoted the next three hours to typing and stuffing envelopes.

CHAPTER 46

Gayle

A few weeks later, Gayle placed the Occupational Outlook Handbook on the table in front of Dani in the local library.

"This handbook lists a lot of different occupations and how much you can expect to be paid," said Gayle.

"That's a big book."

"Maybe you should pick out a couple things you might be interested in and then look up the information."

"Gayle, isn't that James?"

"Where?"

"Walking in the front door?"

Gayle braced herself.

"Yes, that's him," she said trying not to stare.

"I think he's coming over here."

"OK. But you have got to stay focused. You are a senior now and this year is going to go by faster than you think. Why don't you write down a few things you might like to do when you graduate? Then we can take it from there."

"He's coming over here."

"Dani, pay attention," she said firmly, her voice elevated with each word.

James walked over to the table where Gayle and Dani sat.

"Hey, ladies. How are you?" asked James wearing a wide grin.

"Fine," said Gayle.

Dani smiled.

"Hey James."

"Dani, you have grown into a beautiful young lady. I meant to tell you that at the play, but I couldn't get over to you."

"You were there? I did not see you. I was at the door, how did I miss you?"

"Yes, I was there on opening night. I spoke to Mrs. Olivia. Gayle, did she give you my message?"

"No, I'm afraid she didn't."

Dani giggled beneath her breath. Gayle kneed her sister under the table.

"The play was fantastic and I enjoyed it very much. My parents attended the Sunday night show and they said the same thing. You are really a very talented writer."

"Thank you, James. Are you working on lesson plans today?"

"James is a teacher," Gayle said to Dani as if she needed to explain his presence.

"Didn't you go into the Air Force after high school?" asked Dani.

"I sure did. And I went to school while I was in the Air Force."

"Dani is working on college applications and she's not sure what she wants her major to be."

"I completely understand. You'll probably change your mind a few times anyway."

"Gayle said the same thing. Right now I'm thinking about Journalism."

"I'm going to check with the circulation desk and see if they have more college catalogs. I'll be right back," said Gayle, trying to keep Dani focused.

James took the seat at the table in front of Dani.

"So you want to be a writer like your sister?"

"I don't know."

"So who else is here with you? Is Gayle's husband here?" asked James, looking around the library.

"No, he's not here. He went back to New York," said Dani, with a smile. "Does the Air Force help pay for school?"

Joining the Air Force would be one way to get out of town. I would miss my family but I want to get as far away from Samuels as possible.

"They can. Are you interested in the Service?"

"I'm not sure. Where did they send you?"

"I lived in a couple of cities in California. Are you sure you want to live so far away from home?"

Gayle returned to the table with three catalogs in hand.

"They had one for Southern, Louisiana State and Northwestern. I know you said you wanted to go Grambling, but I want you to make sure to look at other options as well."

"How much does college cost?" Dani asked Gayle.

"Don't worry about that right now. Look through these and tell me what interests you."

Dani took the catalogs and Gayle turned to James.

"And you," she said pointing in his direction, "Tell me everything Olivia said to you on opening night."

CHAPTER 47

Dani

A few days later, when Dani and Tasha got home from school Gayle was waiting at the kitchen table with a stack of papers, a Hershey bar, a bag of Doritos and a Coca Cola.

"Hey, Gayle," Dani said.

"Hey, Aunt Gayle," said Tasha giving her a kiss on the forehead. "What are you doing here?"

"I need to go over some paperwork with Dani."

She looked at Dani, winked and tossed the Hershey bar in her direction.

She handed the bag of Doritos to Tasha.

Dani took a seat next to Gayle. Tasha went to the back of the house.

"I made a few copies of the Application for Admission form. Fill one out in pencil and then you can type your answers onto a blank form."

"Can I borrow your typewriter?"

"Of course you can. It is in the car. I was not sure if you would need it today or not. I brought a few stamps because I was not sure how much postage you would need. Two fifteen cent stamps will probably be enough."

"You've thought of everything."

"There's a question on the application about your major to be. Do not sweat it. You'll probably change your mind three or four times before you graduate anyway."

"OK, what else?"

"That's enough for now. But guess what?"

"What?"

"I'm going to throw you a graduation party at my house. You can invite anyone you want."

"A party for me? Really?"

"Yes, for you. I am proud of you, girl. Just let me know how many people will be there. I'll do the rest."

"Okay. Thank you Gayle"

"Stop thanking me and get started on these applications."

Olivia entered the house, still wearing her one-piece orange flame-retardant uniform. She put the hard hat on washroom shelf, and unlaced her steel-toed work boots.

"Hey Olivia," Gayle said.

"Hey, Olivia. How was work?" asked Dani.

"OK. Will one of you take my check to Bossier Bank? I was in such a rush to get home that I drove right by the bank and forgot to stop."

Olivia stood in the washroom taking off her uniform. She placed it in the washer and replaced the jumpsuit with one of the housedresses she kept hanging in the washroom for just this purpose.

"I just want to take a shower and jump in the bed. This is going to have to be an 'eat what you can find' night."

"I'll go."

"The bank closes at five and I need to deposit this check today."

"Yes, ma'am," said Dani.

Olivia added laundry detergent to the washer, and turned the knob to the heavy-duty cycle.

"Thank you. Here are my keys. You can take my car."

She tossed the keys to Dani.

Dani donned a pair of shoes and jumped into the car. She changed the radio from the gospel station to the secular station and headed down Barksdale Boulevard.

That is my song.

She turned up the volume and imagined herself dancing with Mitch at her graduation party. They were laughing and having fun. Her friends commented on what a cute couple they were. She danced in her head as she made her way down Barksdale Boulevard in the middle of five o'clock traffic and right pass Bossier Bank.

I need to turn around and go back. The bank closes at five and I need to hurry.

Dani turned on the signal light and waited so she could cross over the opposite lane and pull into the parking lot of the Barksdale Motel. Then she would merge back into traffic and head toward the bank.

Barksdale Motel had been many things over the years. There were approximately twenty-five rooms on each side of the old gray building. The paint on the outside doors was peeling and a few of the windows were cracked. There were three cars parked in the small lot facing the street. Most of the tenants preferred parking on the other side of the building so they would not be seen.

As she waited, Dani saw a female figure emerge from the rear of Barksdale Motel wearing a cute sleeveless denim jumpsuit, sunglasses and a wide brim hat.

Dani took a second look and realized that the figure was Aretha.

Dani watched as she walked from behind the motel and toward the bank parking space that held her yellow Volkswagen bug.

Then she saw the dark blue Ford Thunderbird with Samuels in the driver's seat pull from the back of the motel.

Dani sat frozen in her car unable to remove her foot from the brake pedal.

She heard a bump and felt a hard hit from the rear of the vehicle.

Olivia's car had been rear-ended.

Samuels turned toward the commotion, looked Dani in the eyes and darted into the oncoming traffic.

CHAPTER 48

Dani

Dani crept into the house.

She found Gayle and Olivia sitting in the kitchen and Dani sensed she had interrupted a private conversation.

Great. They are already in the middle of a drama.

"I didn't make it to the bank," blurted a shaken Dani.

"What?" asked Olivia, turning to look at Dani?

"I had an accident."

Olivia's eyes searched Dani from head to toe. Gayle bolted from her seat.

"What do you mean you had an accident? Are you OK?" asked Olivia sounding a bit confused.

"I'm sorry Olivia. I had an accident in the car. I missed the turn for the bank and I was waiting to turn around when another car ran into the back of your car."

"Are you hurt?" asked Olivia, embracing Dani.

Gayle massaged Dani on the back while Olivia held her.

"No, ma'am, I'm not hurt. I got the other driver's name and address, and stuff. But there's a dent in the car."

Olivia hugged her tighter and then re-inspected her for bruises.

"I'm just glad you're not hurt," Olivia said, placing her arms around Dani again. "Now, let's go take a look at the car."

Dani lead Olivia and Gayle into the garage. Gayle grabbed Dani's hand.

Dani's hand trembled when she pointed to the damage.

She fearfully awaited a response from Olivia.

"It's not that bad," Gayle said.

Olivia nodded in agreement, as she examined the damaged area.

"The insurance should cover it," said Olivia. "We'll take it to Robert Earl this weekend, he should be able to knock that dent right out. Now come on in the house and tell me exactly what happened."

Dani breathed a sigh of relief. She walked inside and prepared to tell Olivia at least most of what happened.

#####

The aroma of Cornish hens, wild rice and mustard greens hit Dani like a ton of bricks when she walked into the house after church. She had not eaten much since the accident two days ago.

"What time does the game come on, Olivia?" asked Leonard.

"I don't know, check the TV guide. It is around here somewhere. I think it comes on at six o'clock," said Olivia.

Leonard pulled himself away from the table with a piece of cornbread in his mouth. He began to search for the TV guide.

Gayle walked in the door with a case of Coca-Cola. She wore a black and white polka dot dressed with big shoulder pads.

"Did ya'll start eating without me?" she asked.

"We sure did, you took too long," Tasha said sticking a slice of Cornish hen in her mouth.

"Come on in and grab a plate," Leonard yelled from the living room.

Gayle kicked off her shoes, washed her hands and grabbed a plate.

"I like that dress, girl. Where'd you find that?" asked Olivia.

The phone rang before Gayle could answer.

Tasha hurried to answer the phone and Gayle sat next to Dani at the table.

"Hello," said Tasha into the phone. " ... Yes, ma'am she is right here. I'll get her for you."

Tasha covered the phone with her hand and turned to Dani, "Aretha's mom wants to talk to you."

"She wants to talk to me?"

Everyone was a little curious as to why Mrs. Mills wanted to talk to Dani. Olivia ruffled her brow and exchanged glances with Leonard.

"She asked for you," Tasha said.

Dani got up from the table and grabbed the phone.

"Hello."

"Dani. This is Mrs. Mills."

"Hello, Mrs. Mills. How are you?"

"I'm fine. Is Aretha still with you?"

"No, ma'am. She's not."

"Do you know where she is?"

"No ma'am, I don't."

"I told her she could spend the night with you last night but she had to come home after church."

"She didn't spend the night over here, Mrs. Mills."

"She didn't?"

"No ma'am, she didn't."

"Was she at church?"

"No ma'am she wasn't."

Leonard lowered the volume on the television and walked into the kitchen.

Everyone was watching Dani and listening to her end of the conversation with Mrs. Mills.

"When was the last time you saw her or talked to her?"

"I think it was Tuesday. Yes, it was Tuesday."

Dani looked at Olivia who was now standing and whispering the name of Jesus.

"If she calls you or if you see her, please let me know."

"Yes, ma'am."

"And tell her she'd better get her butt back here."

"Yes, ma'am."

"What happened?" asked Olivia before Dani could hang up the phone.

"Mrs. Mills wanted to know if Aretha was over here."

"Why? Was she supposed to be over here?" Olivia asked.

"She thought that Aretha had spent the night here last night?"

"Why would she think that?"

"I don't know," said Dani feeling as if she was the one in trouble.

"You mean she has been gone since yesterday?" asked Leonard.

"I think so."

"She wasn't at church today was she?" asked Gayle.

"No."

"Dani, if you know something, you need to let us know," warned Olivia.

"I don't know where she is," said Dani raising her voice only as much as she could get away with.

"I know she's your friend, but don't try to protect her. You need to speak up if you know something," Gayle said.

Dani sighed and rolled her eyes.

"I don't know anything about where Aretha is or where she has been."

Dani grew irritated with their rush to judgment. She really did not know where Aretha was and if she did, she would not tell.

"Did Mrs. Mills call the police?" asked Olivia, taking a sip of Diet Cola.

"I don't know. She didn't say."

"Something doesn't sound right. There has got to be more to this story," said Olivia.

"Has she ever done anything like this before?" asked Gayle.

"I don't think so," said Dani.

"Well, if you talk to her, you need to let her mother know right away," said Olivia.

"Yes, ma'am. I will."

Aretha, I hope you are OK.

First, you meet Samuels at a motel, and then you lie to your mother about spending the night over here. What is going on? More importantly, who are you and what have you done with my best friend?

CHAPTER 49

Dani

Dani sat in her room waiting for the phone to ring. She watched TV for a while, tried on a few outfits, and finally resorted to cleaning up her side of the room. She was running out of ways to keep busy, when the phone rang. She rushed to pick it up on the first ring.

"Hello,"

"Hey, Dani," said Aretha, sounding distraught.

"Aretha, where are you?"

Dani pulled the phone into the closet and sat with her legs crisscrossed.

"I'm at home. Mama told me that she called you."

"Are you OK? Where were you?"

"It doesn't matter. Mama wanted me to call you and let you know that I was back at home."

"We need to talk."

"About what?" asked Aretha.

"I don't know how to say this but I guess I will just come right out and say it."

"What?"

"I saw you and Samuels at the Barksdale Motel on Tuesday. I didn't say anything about that to your mother."

"Yeah and …?"

Dani was not sure if that was anger she detected in Aretha's voice.

"Yeah and he's old enough to be your father."

"Yeah and …?"

"And he's a married man."

"And …"

I think she is angry.

"What about the promise we made to tell each other about the 'first time'?"

"Girl, wake up this is 1981. Do you actually think that people wait for marriage?"

Dani was shocked.

"What?"

Dani stood in the closet cradling the phone on her shoulder and flailing her hands in the air.

"Look, I know you are just jealous because Samuels does not like you. He told me all about how you tried to kiss him at church and how you keep calling him and stuff."

"What? You have got to be kidding me. That is not what happened. He tried to kiss *me*. And he keeps calling *me*."

"If that's true, then why didn't you tell Olivia? I know she would have had him put out of the church for messing with her precious baby sister. I know you are lying. Just admit it, you want him for yourself."

Dani realized she was getting nowhere with Aretha.

"Look, I just wanted to let you know that I saw you and to see if I could help you. That's all."

"If you want to help me, keep your mouth shut or I'll tell what I saw."

"What are you talking about? You didn't see anything."

"Yes, I did. I saw Olivia's car and Deacon Samuels' car leaving the motel when I was at the bank. That is what I saw."

"That was me in Olivia's car, and you know it."

"Ok. Then I saw you and Samuels at the motel. Either way, I was at the bank."

"Why would you do something like that?"

"Because that is my man and this is none of your business," yelled Aretha.

Then all Dani heard was the dial tone.

CHAPTER 50

Dani

The next day after school, Dani tried to focus on her Chemistry homework. Her mind rehearsed last night's conversation with Aretha.

Aretha was right. I should have told Olivia about everything.

"Dani," Olivia yelled from the other room.

"Ma'am?"

"Come here a minute please."

"Yes ma'am."

Dani placed her pencil between the pages of the Chemistry book and closed it. She eased her feet into a pair of slippers and took a quick glance in the mirror on the way out.

Olivia sat on the side of the bed next to the phone.

Dani could tell that something was wrong.

"Ma'am?"

"I just got off the phone with Mrs. Mills."

"What's wrong?"

"Aretha is in the hospital."

"She is? What happened?"

"She took a bunch of sleeping pills. Mrs. Mills came home from work and found Aretha passed out on the floor next to a half-empty bottle of sleeping pills."

Dani stood there looking intently at Olivia but obviously not seeing her.

"The doctor said that she'll be fine. She is conscious, but they're going to keep her in the hospital for a few days."

Dani continued to stare at Olivia.

"Do you know why she would try to hurt herself? Does this have anything to do with why she didn't come home the other night?"

"I don't know."

Dani began to bite her nails.

"If you know something, Dani, please tell me. This is serious. Aretha felt like she needed to take her own life. You're not protecting her by keeping secrets," said Olivia in a small voice, almost pleading.

Dani offered a defensive shrug.

"OK," she said, "Let's say a quick prayer for Aretha and her mother. Then go get your shoes; I'll drive you to the hospital."

#####

Aretha's room was on the second floor near the nurse's station where she lay between the distinctive hospital white sheets and ecru-colored blanket. She wore a look that said she had been through something. Her eyes and face were void of happiness.

Mrs. Mills sat with her shoulder hunched in a chair next to the bed.

"Good evening," Olivia said.

She walked over to Mrs. Mills and gave her a hug.

"Hey," said Mrs. Mills, still dressed in her work clothes. She worked as a cook for Plantation Park Retirement home and wore black pants, a white-collared shirt, hairnet and black rubber-soled shoes.

Dani smiled at her and walked toward Aretha.

"Hey," she said to Aretha, who looked away.

The girls knew it was better not to talk in front of the adults.

Olivia caressed Aretha's hand and said, "You gave us quite a scare."

Mrs. Mills cupped her face with her hands.

Olivia walked over to her, rubbed her on the back. "Let's take a walk. It'll give the girls a chance to talk."

Mrs. Mills stood up, looked at Aretha and walked out of the room. Olivia followed.

CHAPTER 51

Olivia

Joe Ann Mills and Olivia met in high school. They shared a few classes and spent some time together after school when Reverend Ferguson would allow it. Graduation brought marriage for Joe Ann and a ticket to Arizona for Olivia. Joe Ann had been married and divorced by the time Olivia returned to Louisiana. Life had taken them down separate paths.

The women walked silently down the hall. Joe Ann removed a tissue from her pocket and blew her nose.

There was a long pause as they walked down the hall and into the waiting room. They sat on a small sofa near the window.

"Do you feel like talking about it?" asked Olivia.

"Sure," Joe Ann said taking a deep breath. "Aretha asked if she could spend the night with Dani on Saturday. I said OK. They do it all of the time -spend Saturday night at one another's houses and go to church on Sunday morning. I didn't think twice about it because she was going to be at your house."

Mrs. Mills stopped talking and glanced at Olivia for affirmation.

"I don't know. Maybe I should have spent more time at home. There are so many things I could have done differently."

"Joe Ann, don't blame yourself. It's not your fault."

"It's hard when you have to do it all alone, Olivia. She is really a good girl. She made the Honor Roll again, you know."

"I know Joe Ann, I know. Dani told me."

"I worked a double shift Saturday night and I wasn't going to see her until after she came back from church anyway."

"So where did she spend the night?"

"Aretha said she and Dani had an argument so she stayed home instead of going over to your house. She went to church at Lakeside Baptist because she did not want to talk to Dani. Lakeside had a special program and served dinner after the service. That's why she wasn't home when I expected her to be."

Joe Ann hung her head and began to sob.

CHAPTER 52

Dani

"Aretha, what happened?" asked Dani.

Aretha's eyes were heavy.

"Sammy ...Samuels and I had planned to meet at our usual place."

"The Barksdale Motel?"

"Yeah. And when we got there, I told him."

"You told him what?"

Aretha looked Dani in the face and said, "I told him that I was pregnant."

Dani backed away.

"What? You're pregnant?"

"Yes, I am or I was. I lost the baby when I took those pills. Anyway, I told him and he asked me if it was his baby. Can you believe that? He asked me if it was his baby like I was some kind of girl that slept around."

"Aretha, I'm sorry."

"He made me so many promises. He promised to marry me. He promised to leave his wife and marry me. We were going to move to California and live near the rest of his family. Dani, I love him. We were so good together. He was my first."

Dani listened to her friend struggle to breathe between sobs.

"He hasn't called, and I can't call him because his wife might answer the phone."

"Why are you still protecting him, Aretha? You may not believe it now, but he is not the guy for you. God will send someone else for you," Dani said.

"Look, don't start with the God stuff. I have done too many things, things that you do not even know about. I have hurt many people. God will never forgive me and neither should you. Anyway if you really believe all that stuff, why haven't you told Olivia about what Sammy did to you?"

She waited for a response.

Dani had none.

"I had no choice," continued Aretha. "I could not take care of a baby by myself. I could not tell mama. Sammy was not going to help. I just wanted it to all go away. I knew that mama had some sleeping pills in her medicine cabinet. When I got home from school, I took a few. I just wanted it to all go away. The next thing I knew, I was in the hospital."

"I'm so sorry."

Aretha muttered a few words and tears streamed onto her pillow.

Dani fought back tears.

"Right before y'all came in, the doctor told me that I lost the baby. Mama did not even know that I was pregnant. You should have seen the look on her face.

She did not say a word.

She just sat there, staring at the wall.

I messed up. I messed up bad."

Dani reached for a chair and pulled it next to the head of the bed.

"Did you tell her who the father was?" Dani asked.

"No. There's no way I could tell her that."

Dani took a deep breath and said, "Aretha, this has gone too far. It is not worth it. He is not worth it. We have got to tell."

"I can't. If my mama finds out that I have been with a grown man … a grown married man, I do not know what she will do. You can tell Olivia what happened to you, but I am not telling mama. Olivia will pull out the Bible and ask God for direction but my mama will pull out her pistol and ask questions later."

There was a knock at the door.

The pale-lanky woman did not wait for a response before entering the room.

"Good evening, I am Dr. Wimberley from Mental Health Services."

Dr. Wimberley wore a simple long-sleeve, brown dress accessorized only with hospital ID badge and a pair of brown patent-leather pumps. Tiny crow's feet sprouted around her dark-circled eyes.

"You are Aretha Mills?" asked Dr. Wimberley, referencing the medical chart resting in her left hand.

The doctor looked at Dani.

"I'm Dani, Aretha's friend."

"It's nice to meet you Dani. Would you mind giving me a few minutes to chat with Aretha alone?"

"Sure. Aretha, I will call you later. If you need anything before that, just call me."

Aretha nodded.

Dani walked out of the door, down the hall and searched for Olivia and Mrs. Mill. She found them in the waiting room.

"Thanks for coming Dani. You were the one person that Aretha asked to see," said Mrs. Mills.

"You're welcome."

Dani knew she wanted to hear more.

"She didn't say much. I was scared to ask her anything that would make her upset. Then the doctor came in and asked me to leave."

"That was probably her psychiatrist. She wants to talk to Aretha alone first and then she wants to talk to us together," said Mrs. Mills.

"When are they going to let her come home?" asked Olivia.

"They want to make sure she's medically stable, so the doctor is going to run some more test," she paused and looked off into the distance. "They had to pump her stomach ..."

Olivia grabbed Mrs. Mills' hand.

"Dani, would you get Mrs. Mills something to drink?"

"Yes, ma'am."

Dani walked to the nurse's station. The area was busy with papers, machines, and people dressed in white.

"Excuse me. Is there someplace where I can get a drink of water?" asked Dani.

"Yes, sugar, the water fountain is right down the hall to your left," replied an older black woman. She had been reading something from a chart and seemed annoyed to have been disturbed. Her white nurse's pantsuit was spotless and a stethoscope hung around her neck.

"Yes ma'am, I saw the water fountain. But I need to bring something to my friend's mother. Do you have a cup or something I can use?"

The nurse stopped what she was doing and looked into Dani's eyes. Her face softened. "Wait right here, I'll try to find something for you."

A minute later, the nurse returned with a small Styrofoam cup.

"Are you here for the girl in room one thirteen?"

"Yes, ma'am."

"I thought so. I am her nurse. Is her mother all right?"

"Yes, ma'am. She's in the waiting room."

"OK. Let me know if you need anything. My name is Zelma."

"Thank you, Ms. Zelma."

Dani walked away, grateful that Aretha was in the hands of such a caring person. She could hear Olivia praying before she reached the waiting room.

"Heavenly Father, my friend is faced with a difficult situation. Lord, she needs Your strength and You have all the strength she needs.

Lord, there are things happening that we do not understand. But even in the midst of it all, we know that You are Lord.

Father we know that Aretha is troubled.

We ask that you heal her pain. Please stay by her side and comfort both Aretha and Joe Ann. In Jesus' name, Amen."

Dani cleared her throat when she heard Olivia say amen.

"Here you go," she said, handing the cup to Mrs. Mills.

"Thank you, Dani."

Mrs. Mills' hands trembled when she brought the cup to her mouth and sipped of the water.

"Mrs. Mills, the doctor is ready to see you now," said Nurse Zelma from the waiting room door.

"Yes, I will be right there."

"Do you want us to stay?" asked Olivia.

"No. Thank you so much for coming. I didn't know who else to call."

"Do you need us to go by the house and pick up a change of clothes for you?"

"That would be great. My keys are in my purse. And while you're in the house, would you check the messages on the answering machine for me?"

"Sure. Anything else?"

"Just keep us in your prayers."

CHAPTER 53

Olivia

"I'll grab some clothes for Joe Ann, and you grab some things for Aretha," said Olivia when they entered the tiny house.

Dani went to Aretha's room and gathered a few changes of clothes, underwear and a few toiletries. She joined Olivia in Mrs. Mills' room.

"I've got Aretha's stuff. I can help you with Mrs. Mills' things," said Dani.

"Why don't you find an overnight bag or something for us to put these things in?"

"OK."

Dani returned to Aretha's room and grabbed a couple of bags from the back of the closet. She sat on Aretha's bed and turned the first tote inside out. Two pens, a nickel and a couple of pieces of bubblegum tumbled out and onto the bed. Dani looked inside the next tote and found an old photograph. It was a picture of Mrs. Mills and a man sitting on the front porch at Gates of Heaven Baptist Church. Mrs. Mills held a small child in her arms. Dani assumed the child was Aretha.

"Did you find anything?" asked Olivia entering the room.

"Is this a picture of Mr. Mills?"

"Let me see?"

Olivia walked over to the bed and looked at the photo.

"Yeah, that's Joe Ann and that's Buck. He was a big burly fellow. He played football for Charlotte High School."

"Is that Aretha in Mrs. Mills lap?"

"Probably, I moved to Arizona right after they got married. Buck did not stay around too long. He found another woman and they moved away. Be sure and put this picture back where you found it."

"It was in this tote."

"Put it back and let's go."

"Don't forget to check the answering machine."

"Where is it?"

"Mrs. Mills keeps it in her room."

"You're going to have to show me how to do this. I've never worked an answering machine."

Dani put the things back where she found them. They walked back to the master bedroom and over to the night stand where the answering machine rested.

"OK. There are two cassettes. This one has a greeting for people who call the house and this one records the message of the person who is calling," said Dani pointing to each cassette.

"So how do I get the messages?"

"You just push this button right here and after it rewinds, you push play."

Olivia grabbed a pen and a piece of paper from her purse. She wrote down the names, telephone numbers and messages of two bill collectors, a cousin from Houston and a man asking Joe Ann out on a date.

CHAPTER 54

Gayle

The responses to Gayle's query letters were positive. She even received a few calls requesting a copy of her script and one was ready to fax over the legal documents.

Now it was a matter of waiting on an offer.

She decided it was a good time to clean the refrigerator, something she had wanted to do for weeks. She took a sip of her coffee and began emptying the contents and tossing anything past its prime.

I wonder how long eggs can stay fresh in the refrigerator. Gayle removed a carton of eggs. *I think these have been in here since William left.*

She removed the drawers, placed them in the sink and filled them with warm soapy water. As she washed the drawers, the phone rang. Gayle dried her hands with a paper towel and reached for the kitchen phone.

"Hello,"

"Hey Gayle, this is Olivia."

"Good. You're just the person I needed to talk to."

"Why? What's wrong?"

"I wanted to know how long eggs stay fresh in the refrigerator."

"I'm not sure. How long have you had them in there?"

"I don't remember, but I think I bought them before the opening of the play."

Gayle could hear Olivia laughing.

"Well if you're not sure how long you've had them then you've probably had them too long. I'd throw them out if I were you."

"I was afraid you were going to say that."

"Look, I wanted to know if you had a chance to talk to Dani yet."

"Not yet. Why?"

"Well things have gotten worse."

"What happened?"

"I can't really say but I think we should do what we can to find out if Dani is involved."

"Involved in what?"

"I can't say, but just find out what she knows about Aretha. She's in her room now if you want to call her when we get off the phone."

"You're scaring me."

"Just see what you can find out, OK. By the way, do you have an answering machine?"

"Sure do. Are you thinking about getting one?"

"I was thinking about it."

"I love mine. I use it for business, so I don't miss a writing assignment."

"Are they expensive?"

"You can probably get one from Sears for about a hundred dollars."

"I am going to ask Leonard to get one for us."

"Well, welcome to the eighties."

Gayle laughed but Olivia did not find the humor.

"Let me finish cleaning my refrigerator. I promise to call Dani but I'm not promising to tell you anything we discuss unless I think she's in trouble."

"Thanks, Gayle."
"OK, Bye."

CHAPTER 55

Olivia

The aroma of fresh brewed coffee drifted to the back of the house and brought Leonard to the kitchen, the next morning. He found Olivia at the kitchen table absorbed in reading the morning paper.

Leonard pulled two mugs from the cupboard and poured two cups of coffee.

"How'd things go at the hospital yesterday?"

"Aretha's probably going to be in there a couple more days. Joe Ann is a mess. She is trying to hold it together. But I cannot say that I blame her. I would probably be the same way."

Leonard placed the two cups of coffee on the table and sat next to his wife.

Olivia told Leonard about how Joe Ann found Aretha passed out on the floor after school.

"Bless her heart," said Leonard.

"I think Dani knows more than she's willing to share."

"Be careful. If she doesn't know anything and you accuse her, it could do more harm than good."

"I'm not going to say anything. It will all come out eventually. By the way, we went by Joe Ann's house to get them a change of clothes. Joe Ann asked me to check her phone messages while I was there."

"She has one of those telephone answering machines?"

"Yeah, have you ever seen one?"

"I've seen the commercials."

"It's a handy little machine. I think we should get one."

"Why do we need an answering machine when we have two teenagers in the house?"

"We need an answering machine so we can get all of our messages and not just half of them."

"Or get them two or three days after the person calls," Leonard added with a chuckle. "I'll stop by the store and look at one after work. I will let you know. Now please pass the sports section?"

CHAPTER 56

Dani

Dani proceeded straight to her closet after school and called the hospital. Tasha sat in the living room with a bag of Doritos and a glass of grape Kool-Aid watching an ABC After-School Special.

"Mental Health Nurse's station, may I help you?"

"Yes, I'd like to have Aretha Mills' room please,"

"I'm sorry but she's still unable to receive phone calls."

"OK, thank you."

Dani hung up the phone and stared at the big red letter "F" on her Chemistry Exam. She expected the poor grade.

I got exactly what I deserved. If I could do it all over again, I would tell everything from the beginning. I would tell Olivia that Samuels touched me. I would tell that he grabbed me and tried to kiss me. I would tell Olivia about the night of the play and about Samuels parking near my school and about the times he called the house. Maybe if I had not kept quiet, Aretha would not be in the hospital.

The telephone rang as she fought back tears.

"Hello."

"Hey Dani, its Gayle."

"Hey Gayle."

"You sound sad. Is everything all right?"

"Not really, I made an F on my Chemistry exam."

"Chemistry is not an easy subject. What's your average in the class?"

"It's probably a high D or a low C."

"How long have you been having trouble in the class? Have you talked to your teacher?"

"I just don't get chemistry, that's all. The teacher gave me some extra problems to work on, but that didn't help much."

"Maybe you should get a tutor."

"Maybe."

"Is everything else all right? Did you and Aretha work out your issues? I know you said that the two of you had a fight."

"Yeah, we're fine."

"Loretta and I have arguments all the time. I think our last one was about something silly. What did you and Aretha argue about?"

"I don't even remember."

Dani wanted to get off the phone. Gayle was asking too many questions.

"Gayle, can I call you back. I should probably get started on my homework."

"Sure honey. I will talk to you later. Call me if you feel like talking."

Two minutes later the phone rang again. She let Tasha answer this time.

"Dani, the phone's for you. It's Mitch," yelled Tasha from the living room.

Dani grabbed the phone, which was still sitting on the bed where she had left it.

"Hello."

"Hey Dani, What's up?"

"Hey Mitch, not much."

"I just heard that Aretha was in the hospital. Is that true?"

"Yeah, she's in the hospital."

"Is she alright? What happened?"

"I have not talked to her today, but yesterday she was doing better. Look, I really cannot talk right now. Is it alright if I call you back?"

"Sure. If you talk to Aretha, tell her I hope she gets better soon."

"I will. Talk to you later."

She disconnected the call and the phone rang again.

"Hello," she said answering before the first ring was complete.

"Hello," said the caller.

Dani recognized Samuels's voice on the line and she began to tremble.

"Hello," he repeated.

"Why don't you just leave me alone? Haven't you caused enough trouble?"

"Trouble? You do not know what trouble is sweetheart. Now shut up and listen."

Dani stood frightened and quiet.

"If you breathe a word of what you know, I'll make so much trouble for you and your entire family you won't know what hit you," he growled.

He must have spoken to Aretha. She told him about our visit to the hospital.

"Leave my family out of this. What does my family have to do with this?"

"What does your family have to do with this? Wasn't it Olivia's car that Aretha saw at Barksdale Motel?"

"Yes, it was Olivia's car. But she was not in it! You saw me when you pulled out of the parking lot like a coward."

"Watch your mouth little girl."

"I know about you and Aretha. I know that you've been meeting her there and that Barksdale Motel is your little hideaway, you pervert."

"What I do is my business. I'm a grown man, sweetheart."

"You're a grown man that got a teenage girl pregnant and made her try to kill herself."

"I didn't make her do anything. And how do you know it was my baby anyway? We will never know will we? Now shut up and listen. I've been thinking about the time we shared in the closet during the play."

"You mean when you molested me?"

"I wouldn't call it that. I had a good time, didn't you?"

"Are you out of your mind? You dragged me in there against my will. If I hadn't kicked you ..."

"That's where you messed up. Nobody and I mean nobody does that to me and gets away with it. And if you repeat a single word of what happened in that closet to anyone, including Olivia, I will kill you. I know where you live. I know where you go to school and I know where you go to church," he said with a laugh. "Now get in your car and meet me at Barksdale Motel so we can finish what we started."

"Are you crazy? I'm not meeting you anywhere."

"You will or I'll make your precious Olivia's life a living hell. Now get in the car and meet me in thirty minutes."

"I can't just leave the house. We're not allowed to leave without telling Olivia where we're going."

"Tell her you're going to the library or something. I do not care. Just be at Barksdale Motel room one twenty-six in thirty minutes," ordered Samuels before hanging up the phone.

Dani hung up the receiver and stood paralyzed.

She looked at the alarm clock on her nightstand. It read five fifteen.

She had no way of knowing that the new answering machine had recorded the entire conversation.

CHAPTER 57

Olivia

Olivia was in no mood to handle the traffic congestion on I-20.

I think I climbed every tower in the refinery to install, test, and repair or maintain a piece of equipment today.

She turned on the radio and laughed when she heard the announcer say that he would be playing Tramaine Hawkin's *Change* after the break. Olivia loved the words of that song and it always ministered to her but the song also reminded her of Dani's attempt at singing a solo in church.

She chuckled and passed a slow moving eighteen-wheeler.

I need to wash at least one load of clothes before I go to bed, and there is a load in the dryer I need to fold. What are we eating for dinner?

When she finally made it home Olivia entered the washroom and removed her dirty uniform. She placed it in the washer and added more than the usual amount of laundry detergent.

It had been a hard day.

She put on a housedress.

She noticed Tasha sleeping on the couch next to an empty glass and bag of Doritos.

How many times have I asked them not to eat in the living room?

She was just about to wake Tasha and scold her about eating in the living room when she remembered Aretha lying in her hospital bed.

She stood watching Tasha sleep and realized how blessed she was to have two happy, healthy girls.

"Lord, please bless both Joe Ann and Aretha."

She walked to the back of the house and she literally ran into Dani in the hallway.

"Slow down, little girl. What's the hurry?"

"Olivia, I just tried to call you at work. Is it OK if I run over to the library? I'm supposed to meet a couple of friends there for a study group?" said a panicky Dani.

"Sure, go to the library. You want to take my car?"

"No thanks."

"Have you talked to Aretha today?"

"No, she still can't receive phone calls."

"I wonder how Joe Ann's doing. Maybe we can ride over there when you get back from the library. What do you think?"

Dani looked away hoping the conversation would not be a long one.

"OK, sure."

Dani began gnawing away at her nails like a beaver on a piece of wood.

"What's wrong with you? Why do you look so nervous?"

"I'm not sure what time the library closes."

"OK, go. Be careful and do not forget your jacket. It's a little chilly out there."

"Yes ma'am."

Dani grabbed a windbreaker and proceeded out of the door. Olivia went to her bedroom.

It has been a long day. Maybe I will treat myself to a relaxing bath instead of a quick shower.

Olivia began to search bathroom cabinets for the bath oils that Gayle gave her for Christmas last year. She had graciously thanked Gayle, but stored the oils away because she was in the habit of taking showers. She found the package of bath oils in the back of the cabinet tucked behind the surplus bars of soap, toothpaste and rolls of toilet paper.

Olivia put the tub stopper into the drain and started running the water making sure it was a comfortable temperature. She poured the lavender bath oil under the running water and watched the bath oils foam. A cloud of lavender took over the room. The fragrance was heavenly. She gathered her clothes and a couple of towels. She turned off the water when it was deep enough to submerge her whole body. For the next twenty minutes, Olivia shut out the rest of the world as the soothing lavender oils penetrated deep into her skin tissue and provided much needed rejuvenation.

CHAPTER 58

Gayle

This house is cleaner today than it was the day we moved in.

During the last weeks, she had cleaned the refrigerator, washed the windows, painted the front door and scrubbed all the baseboards. She could have easily hired someone to do the manual labor, but being busy kept her mind occupied while she waited to hear back from the studios regarding her screenplay.

She sat on her couch enjoying a cup of her favorite French vanilla flavored coffee.

Dani is definitely keeping something from us. Her loyalty to Aretha is admirable but if the secret is something so severe that it caused Aretha to be hospitalized, then we might have a problem.

Gayle took a sip of coffee and pulled her feet beneath her on the couch. She reached for one of her many blank notebooks and began writing.

Her mind traveled back to Parkway High School. She remembered when she did not want to share anything with Daddy or Gertrude and the diary was her only friend. Gayle jotted a few notes and returned the coffee cup to the kitchen.

If I leave now, maybe I can get to Dani before Olivia comes home and we will have a chance to talk privately.

She grabbed for the keys and the phone rang.

I had better answer that in case it is about my screenplay. "Hello."

"Hey Gayle, its Loretta."

"What's happening, Lo?"

"Not much down here. I was thinking about coming up for a visit this weekend. Do you have plans?"

"No, I don't. You know you are welcome to visit anytime."

"Thanks. Have you heard anything back about the screenplay?"

"No, not yet."

"I hate waiting. Somebody has got to make an offer soon."

"I know. I have been doing a little bit of everything to keep myself busy and to keep my mind occupied. I even cleaned out the refrigerator the other day."

"Does William know you're waiting on an offer?"

"No, why?"

Gayle frowned, dropped her keys on the table and sat back down on the sofa.

"Have you thought about what you'll do when you get an offer?"

"What are you talking about?"

"Money can bring out the worst in people."

"And?"

"And people get funny when money is involved. If you're thinking about divorcing him, now is the time to do it."

"I never said I was thinking about divorce. Why would you even bring that up?" asked Gayle, beginning to grow a little irritated.

"First of all, how faithful do you think he's being two thousand miles away from you? Secondly, you are headed for the big time and when you arrive, he will try to take you for all that you have worked so hard to achieve. You have got to get a lawyer and get one soon."

"Look, leaving is not as easy as you think."

"Evidently, it was easy for him. How long has he been gone?"

"You don't understand. When I said until death do us part, I meant it."

"I'm just trying to look out for you. You have been dreaming of this since we met at Grambling. You deserve to be happy. Are you happy, Gayle? Are you really happy?"

Gayle refused to answer.

"And how long has it been since the two of you …you know …?

"That is none of your business!"

"Things probably got pretty hot and heavy when he came home for opening night, but how long before that?"

Gayle thought back to opening night. She and William spent the night addressing envelopes to production companies.

Could it be that the thought addressing envelopes was more appealing to him than spending a night of passion with his wife? Of course not. He helped me with my project. He was being thoughtful, wasn't he?

"That's enough, Lo. I am not having this discussion with you. I gotta go check on Dani."

"Ok, that's cool. What's wrong with Dani?"

"Not sure. Her friend Aretha is in the hospital. Something is going on and Olivia is worried about Dani. I promised to see what I could find out."

"Do you think something is going on?"

"I kind of do. I tried to talk to her about it earlier, but she is not letting go of much information."

"Why is her friend in the hospital? What happened to her?"

"Don't know."

"You don't know a lot of stuff, huh?"

"Lo ..."

"Fine, you don't have to talk to me about it. However, you do need to talk to a lawyer about it. Do you have one? Do you want me to find one for you?"

"No thank you. I gotta run. I'll call you later."

"OK, bye but think about what I said."

CHAPTER 59

Dani

Dani prayed for courage.

"Lord, I know I've done some stupid things. I go to church every Sunday even if it is because Olivia makes us go. I read my Bible every day and it is not because Olivia makes me. I know I was curious about sex, but I was not really going to do it. Lord, if you get me out of this, I promise to wait until I get married to have sex. Please give me strength and courage and have mercy on me, in Jesus name, amen."

Dani drove around to the back of the dilapidated Barksdale Motel. She parked in front of room one twenty-six. She reached in her pocket to make sure the knife she had taken from the kitchen drawer was still in place and she got out of the car.

She stood for a few seconds without moving, and then she knocked on the door. Samuels appeared wearing jeans, a navy-blue velour V-neck sweater, and a lascivious grin.

He waved her into the room and surveyed the parking. Samuels chuckled at Dani's naivety when he saw her bright orange Vega parked right in front of his motel room door.

Dani entered the smoke-filled room and looked around. This was her first time in a motel. The congested room held with a queen-sized bed, a small wooden dresser with a television, and a tiny desk with a flimsy chair. The stout smell of liquor penetrated the room.

She stood next to the door hugging her purse to her chest and staring at the faded green carpet. She watched a large cockroach make its way across the floor.

Samuels sat on the bed and tapped the space next to him as if to say, "Have a seat".

The bed creaked when he moved.

Dani did not move.

"Well at least take off that jacket," he slurred.

Dani still did not respond.

"We can do this the easy way or we can do this the hard way. It is all up to you. Now take off your jacket and sit down."

Dani carefully removed her jacket hoping the knife would remain safely tucked inside the pocket. She sat down in the chair holding both her jacket and her purse.

She avoided eye contact and continued to study the cockroach that was now crawling toward the bed.

Samuels stood and pulled the chair with Dani in it closer to the edge of the bed where he stared at her as if she was a mouth-watering rib-eye steak.

Dani trembled.

"You are so beautiful," he whispered as he licked his lips and rested one hand on her thigh.

Dani pushed his hand away.

Samuels laughed and reached for the bottle of Jack Daniels sitting on the dresser desk next to the bed. He removed the lid and took a swallow.

He grimaced.

"Have some?" he asked, extending the bottle toward her.

"No, thank you."

"No, have some," he repeated. This time it was an order and not a query.

Dani took the bottle and slowly brought it to her mouth. The stench singed the inside of her nostrils. The liquor burned the inside of her mouth and throat when she swallowed.

She scowled.

He laughed.

"You'll get used to it soon enough. Take another swallow."

Dani did as instructed.

She thought her insides would spontaneously combust.

He took the bottle.

"That's enough for now."

Samuels stuck the bottle in his mouth, took a large swallow of the dark liquid and screwed the cap back on.

His eyes never left Dani.

Samuels stood up, grabbed her shoulders and pulled Dani to his chest.

Her jacket and purse fell to the floor.

She looked to see if the knife was visible.

It was not.

Samuels pushed the chair against the wall. Dani reached for her jacket.

"You won't need that," he said, taking the jacket and throwing it across the room. The jacket soared through the air and the knife plunged onto the floor.

"What were you planning to do with that," he asked angrily picking up the knife. He backhanded her across the face. She fell on the bed.

Her head exploded in pain.

He reached between the mattresses and pulled out a gun.

"I hoped we could get through this without my friend here," he said referring to the gun.

CHAPTER 60

Olivia

Olivia changed into a pair of sweatpants and a t-shirt.

That was a nice bath. I should do that more often. I feel so much better.

She checked the time and saw the answering machine sitting next to the alarm clock on the nightstand.

The phone rang before she could check the messages.

"Hello?"

"Hey, honey. How are you?" asked Leonard.

"I'm great. I took a nice relaxing bath."

"Wow. You have not done that in a long time. What's the occasion?"

"It was one of those days at work today."

"Well, I'm glad to see you taking care of yourself. How about I stop and pick up dinner so you won't have to worry about cooking."

"You know that might not be such a bad idea. Just get a burger and fries for everybody. You probably ought to get a couple of extra burgers just in case. And don't forget that Tasha doesn't like pickles."

"OK, anything else?"

"No, I don't think so. We have drinks here."

"Have you tried the new answering machine?"

"Not yet. I'll check when I hang up the phone with you."

"OK. Then I will let you go. I'll be home soon."

"OK. Bye."

"Bye."

Olivia hung up the phone and looked at the machine.

I suppose it is just like the one at Joe Ann's house, she thought as she turned the dial to the left.

There were two hang-ups and then she heard Dani talking to Gayle.

"Leonard must have hooked this up the wrong way. We're supposed to be able to listen to messages from people calling us and not us talking to callers," Olivia said to herself. "He's going to have to fix that tonight."

She laughed and listened to Dani tell Gayle about the F in Chemistry. Olivia was disappointed that Gayle was unable to glean more information about Aretha.

She smiled when she heard the conversation between Mitch and Dani.

Then she heard his voice. She recognized it right away. She was still and quiet as the voices rang from the machine.

She heard Samuels's threats and Dani's pleas. Olivia listened to Samuels admitting to molesting Dani.

She heard him confess to possibly fathering Aretha's baby.

Then she heard Samuels tell Dani to meet him at Barksdale Motel in thirty minutes and to lie about going to the library.

"The library?" she said to herself, "That's where Dani said she was going."

Olivia ran to her closet and put on a pair of sneakers.

What time did Dani leave?

It was before I took that stupid bath, what was I thinking?

Olivia ran down the hall and into the living room shouting, "Tasha, Tasha wake up."

"Ma'am?"

"I need you to call your daddy for me. Tell him to meet me at Barksdale Motel."

"Why?"

"Just do what I told you to do!"

Tasha picked up the phone and began dialing her father's work number. Olivia grabbed the black, cast-iron skillet.

"There was no answer," said Tasha, entering the kitchen where she saw her mother holding the skillet.

Olivia placed the skillet on the counter, grabbed a piece of paper and a pen and began writing.

"Give this note to him as soon as he walks in the door. Do you hear me? As soon as he walks in the door," she ordered, her voice rising with every word.

"Ok, I will. What is wrong mama? Where are you going with that skillet?"

"Stop asking questions. Just give that note to your daddy," said Olivia as she ran out of the door.

Olivia drove fifty miles an hour through the residential neighborhood dodging a couple of kids playing in the street.

I have got to get there before it is too late.

She turned onto Barksdale Boulevard and found herself driving behind a slow-moving horse-trailer. She put on her turn signal and got into the right lane but traffic was back-to-back. She was forced to drive the forty-five mile an hour speed limit that meant she would also be forced to meet every red light until she made it to Barksdale Motel.

After the third light, Olivia pulled into the parking lot of Barksdale Motel and drove around the building until she saw Dani's orange Chevy Vega parked right in front of the peeling red door to room one twenty-six.

CHAPTER 61

Gayle

Gayle pulled into the driveway as Leonard was bringing the burgers in the house.

"Olivia's not cooking tonight huh?" asked Gayle taking the bag of French fries from Leonard.

"No, I was surprised she asked me to pick up the burgers and fries. I do not know where she went. Her car is not here."

"She'll probably be right back."

Leonard secured the bottom of the bag of burgers with his left arm, shut the car door with his foot and followed Gayle into the house."

Tasha ran into the kitchen.

"Slow down little girl. Where did your mama go so fast?"

"I don't know, but she told me to give you this note as soon as you walked in the house."

Leonard placed the bag of burgers on the kitchen counter and took the note from Tasha.

"Go ahead and grab a burger. There are a couple of burgers in there without pickles," he said.

Tasha searched the bag for her pickle-less burger and Leonard turned his attention to the note.

Leonard, listen to the answering machine and
meet me at the Barksdale Motel, room one-twenty-six
as soon as possible.

Leonard dropped the note on the counter and rushed to the back of the house.

"Leonard, what's wrong?" asked Gayle.

"I'm not sure. Read the note."

Gayle read the note and followed Leonard to the master bedroom.

They listened to the answering machine.

They heard the two hang-ups.

They heard Dani tell Gayle about the F in Chemistry. Leonard realized that he had programed the answering machine to record the phone conversations and he laughed at himself.

Gayle covered her mouth and tried not to laugh.

"I know what Dani's going to be working on tonight," said Leonard.

Gayle smiled and said, "And I know what you'll be working on tonight," she said pointing to the answering machine.

They listened to the conversation between Mitch and Dani, but it was the next conversation that left them dumbfounded.

Leonard headed for the door as soon as the conversation ended.

"Call the police!" he said while running out of the door.

Gayle picked up the phone and dialed the number to the police department.

"Bossier City Police Department, what is your emergency?"

"There's going to be a murder at Barksdale Motel room one-twenty six. Send someone over there fast!"

CHAPTER 62

Olivia

"Samuels open this door or I'll knock it down!"

Olivia knocked on the motel door so loud that the person in the next room looked out of his window to see what was going on. The onlooker quickly retreated behind the curtain to avoid being recognized.

"Samuels, I know you're in there. Now open this door!

Olivia tried to look through the filthy window hoping to be able to see inside. She kicked an empty Budweiser can sitting in front of the window.

"Samuels, open this door!"

Samuels opened the door with the gun in his hand.

"Shut up and get in here!" he ordered.

Olivia stepped into the room and Samuels closed the door behind her.

She could smell alcohol.

"Now drop the skillet."

Olivia dropped the skillet and ran over to Dani who was sprawled on the bed, fully clothed but unconscious.

Olivia sat on the bed and gently placed Dani's head in her lap.

"What did you do to her?"

"I think she had a little too much to drink," he said pointing to the bottle of Jack Daniels and laughing.

"Are you crazy? You gave her alcohol?"

"It's not necessary to call names, Ms. Olivia."

Olivia pulled Dani into her arms. She noticed the swelling around her eye.

"Dani, wake up baby. It's Olivia."

Samuels laughed.

Olivia looked at Samuels standing there holding the gun.

If looks could kill, Samuels would have been six feet under at that moment.

"What is wrong with you, man? Do you get your thrills from hurting little girls? This is a child and she needs a doctor. Call an ambulance."

Samuels ignored her plea.

Olivia laid Dani's head gently on the bed. She stood, faced Samuels and slowly walked toward him.

"I said she needs a doctor."

"Shut up. Do you see this gun in my hand?"

He slapped Olivia across her face. Her vision blurred from the impact. Olivia attempted to kick him in his groin. Samuels dodged the kick and followed with a blow that knocked her to the floor.

CHAPTER 63

Dani

Dani heard voices in the background and she tried to part her weighty eyelids.

"You didn't think you could overpower me did you? Now get up," said Samuels pointing the gun at Olivia.

Olivia stood to her feet. She could taste the blood inside her mouth.

"Look, if you walk out now, no one has to know what happened," said Olivia. She would definitely deal with Samuels later. Dani was her priority right now.

Dani began to stir.

Am I dreaming or is Olivia here?

"Do you think I'm a fool?" said Samuels, his voice angered.

"You're a fool who preys on little girls."

Samuels backhanded Olivia just as he had done earlier to Dani.

The gun fell to the floor.

Samuels commenced with vicious kicks to her rib.

Dani fought to regain consciousness.

I am coming Olivia. I will help.

Dani willed herself to move.

She resisted the heaviness of her body and pulled herself into a seated position.

The energy drained from her like air escaping a balloon.

She battled the urge to lie back down.

Her right eye throbbed and refused to open.

With one eye, she watched as Samuels raised his right foot and plowed it into Olivia's side.

Dani was determined to make the ten-mile stretch from the bed to the gun. She struggled to her feet, reached down on the floor and snatched the gun. She was barley conscience but she aimed the gun in his direction.

Samuels stopped when he saw Dani with the gun.

"What are you going to do, shoot me?" he asked.

There was a loud pop and Samuels fell to the floor.

"Police! Open up!"

The door flew open and two armed police officers entered.

"Drop your weapons!"

Olivia stood over Samuels with a bloody cast iron skillet.

Dani stood frozen with the gun in her hand.

Olivia dropped the skillet to the floor.

"Drop the gun Dani. It's all over," said Olivia.

Dani responded to the sound of Olivia's voice and dropped the gun. One of the officers confiscated the skillet and the gun. The other handcuffed Samuels and placed him in the back seat of the squad car.

CHAPTER 64

Gayle

Leonard, Gayle and Tasha gathered in the master bedroom after Dani and Olivia's release from the emergency room that night. Olivia insisted that Dani sleep in the bed with her.

"I want to be with her when she wakes up," said Olivia, barely touching reality herself.

Leonard did not want to upset his wife and he gave in to her demand without a fight. He unplugged the phone and the answering machine.

"No phone calls or visitors for the next few days. Olivia and Dani need to rest," he said to Tasha and Gayle.

Gayle sat in a chair in the corner of the room and Tasha sat at the foot of the bed watching her mother.

"Don't forget the police will be here in the morning to question them," said Gayle.

"That's right. No one is to talk to Olivia or Dani unless I'm in the room," said Leonard.

"I'm going to spend the night over here. Can I sleep in your room with you Tasha?" asked Gayle.

Tasha nodded.

The room was silent for a few minutes. Everyone watched the patients as they slept.

"She tried to tell me about Samuels and I didn't believe her," said Leonard shaking his head. "She had a bad feeling about him from the beginning. She did not even want him to be at the youth meetings. I should have listened to her."

"She tried to tell me the same thing. She asked me to keep him away from the girls during the play," said Gayle.

"I should have broken his neck when I saw him come out of that motel room," said Leonard.

"I need to run home, but I'll be right back. Do you want to go with me, Tasha?"

"No thank you. I want to stay here with mama and Dani."

"It's time for you to get to bed too," said Leonard.

"Can I sleep in here, Daddy?"

"There's no room."

"I can sleep on the floor."

"No, honey I don't think so."

"Tasha, are you going to make me sleep in your room by myself?" asked Gayle.

Gayle looked at her watch.

"I'll be back in less than an hour. Take your bath and put on your pajamas. I'll be back before you fall asleep."

"OK."

"Leonard have you eaten anything?"

Olivia began to stir.

Leonard held his index finger to his mouth indicating that they should speak softer.

"No, I'll grab one of those burgers in a few minutes," he whispered.

"Those burgers are probably mushy by now. I will pick up something on my way back. I need to check my messages and grab a few things. Do you need anything else while I'm out?"

"No, thank you."

Leonard plopped down into the chair as soon as Gayle got up. He planned to sit there until the sun came up the next morning.

Gayle got in her car and drove across the bridge. She was still in shock and could not believe how things had transpired so quickly.

Gayle made it home, packed an overnight bag and listened to her answering machine in less than an hour. When she returned to Olivia's, everyone was asleep. She decided to wait until Olivia and Dani were feeling better before telling them about the incredible offer she received from Disney to buy her screenplay.

CHAPTER 65

Gayle

Leonard walked into the house after church and removed his gray suit jacket. He worried how the news of Samuels' bail would affect Olivia and Dani.

"Hey, Leonard. I hope you like lasagna," Gayle said.

She stood at the kitchen sink washing a pot. Basil, oregano and garlic permeated the room. "If it tastes anything like it smells, I'm sure I'll love it. How are the patients?" he asked, loosening his tie and undoing the top button of his shirt.

"They're fine. Dani is sleeping. Olivia is awake. She is back there talking to Tasha. They have been back there a while. I think Olivia is getting tired of lying around. You know how she likes to keep busy."

Gayle placed the pot under running water and rinsed off the suds.

"Yeah, I don't know how much longer we can get her to keep still. It is just not in her nature. Were you able to get them to eat anything this morning?"

"Olivia had a little oatmeal. Dani did not want anything. The pain is stealing her hunger. Did the pastor hold the meeting with the congregation after church today?"

Gayle placed the pot in the dish strainer and grabbed another dirty dish.

"Yeah. People had already heard the rumors."

"Were any names mentioned?"

"No. But it was obvious that my family was missing. People will figure it out. Samuels is out on bail you know."

Gayle dropped the dish she was washing in the sink and turned toward Leonard.

"No, I didn't know. How had he managed that? How much was his bail?"

"I'm not sure. Maybe he has some money somewhere that we don't know about or maybe he has someone helping him."

Gayle shook her head in amazement.

"Wait until Olivia finds out."

"Wait until Olivia finds what out?" said Olivia slowly making her way through the living room and into the kitchen, her body still aching from combat. She wore a two-piece white nylon tricot knit pajama set with nylon satin eyelet neckline.

Tasha followed close behind.

Tasha hugged her father, "Hey Daddy. How was church?"

"It was good, baby."

Leonard helped Olivia to the table, "What are you doing out of bed?"

"I've been in bed for four days. I need to move around. Now what are you waiting for me to find out?"

Leonard and Gayle swapped a look that told Olivia she needed to have a seat.

Tasha pulled out a seat from the kitchen table and motioned for her mother to sit down.

"Samuels is out on bail," said Leonard.

Olivia took a minute to digest the news. She placed her elbows on the table and her head in her hands.

"He's out of jail?" asked Tasha.

"Just until the trial is over, there's no way he can weasel out of prison after the trial," said Leonard.

"But what if he tries to come after Mama or Dani again?" asked Tasha.

"He won't," Olivia reassured Tasha, "He's smart enough not to do anything that stupid. If he tries to mess with me or mine, I'll make him wish he hadn't."

Leonard looked at his wife, "Calm down Olivia."

"I am calm," said Olivia, with an expression opposite of calm on her face.

"Gayle, make sure all of the skillets are locked away," teased Leonard.

The room exploded with laughter.

"Don't make me laugh, it hurts," said Olivia grasping her bandaged side.

"Sorry, Baby."

"Hey Olivia, I made lasagna. Do you think we can get Dani to eat some?"

"I'll make her eat some even if it's just a spoonful. She can't take her medicine on an empty stomach," said Olivia.

"Are you going to tell her that Samuels is out on bail?" asked Gayle.

"I am not sure. She is frightened as it is. I cannot move without her being underfoot. The only reason she is not in here now is because she is asleep."

"She needs some things to keep her mind occupied. Did the doctor say how much longer she should stay in bed?" asked Leonard.

"He said she would heal physically and emotionally at her own pace. He said we shouldn't push her to talk about what happened."

The doorbell rang and the conversation came to a halt.

"I'll get it. It is too soon for Dani or Olivia to have visitors. Whoever this is will have to come back some other time," said Leonard.

The others listened to see how Leonard was going to get rid of the unanticipated guest.

"Well, look who's here," said Leonard in a tone that let the rest of the family know the visitor was welcomed.

"Hello Leonard. How are you? Is Gayle over here?" said the familiar deep-baritone voice.

Gayle opened the oven to check on the lasagna. When she heard the visitor's voice, she slammed the oven shut.

"Is that William?" Gayle asked herself.

They had talked to each other every night since the attack. He listened closely when she rehashed every moment of the ordeal. William ended each call with a prayer for Olivia, Dani and the rest of the family. He had mentioned that he was going to try to get down to Louisiana, but Gayle did not expect to see him so soon.

Tasha ran to greet him at the door.

Leonard, William and Tasha walked into the living room. William wore acid-washed jeans and a black Members Only jacket. He held two dozen roses in his arms: one dozen for Olivia and one dozen for Dani.

"Ali!" he jokingly called out to Olivia.

Then he placed a kiss on her forehead and handed her the roses.

"Thank you, William. Tasha, would you put this in a vase for me."

Tasha took the roses from her mother and went to look for a vase.

"And these are for Dani," he said referring to the second bouquet.

"Tasha, would you put these in water for Dani, too?"

"Yes, ma'am," said Tasha, feeling a bit encroached upon.

"I have something else for you, but you've got to promise me one thing," William said, turning to Olivia.

"What's that?"

"If you ever have the urge to come after me with a skillet at least give me a warning?"

Everyone in the room broke out in laughter.

Olivia clenched her side as she chuckled.

Gayle walked over to her husband and gave him a generous hug.

"I'm glad you're here," she whispered in his ear.

He smiled and gave her a sensuous kiss in return.

Everyone took a seat at the dining room table.

"How's Dani?" asked William.

"She's getting better. She's been through a lot," said Gayle.

"This whole family has been through a lot," said William, shaking his head in disbelief. "I've never met a stronger group of people in my life."

The room grew still, everyone lost in their own thoughts.

"Is that my wife's lasagna I smell?" asked William intentionally breaking the silence.

"It sure is," said Gayle.

"When do we eat?" asked William.

William watched his wife bring plates and silverware to the table. He thought about how much he missed her.

"I need to wash my hands," he said and headed for the bathroom in the back of the house.

Gayle removed the lasagna from the oven, cut it into sections and dug out portions for each plate. She placed a bowl of tossed salad on the table and gave everyone a glass of ice tea.

When William returned, Leonard returned to the table and blessed the food.

"How long do you get to stay this time, Uncle William?" asked Tasha stringing a long-gooey piece of hot cheese from her plate to her fork.

"I asked for a week off. I thought that maybe I could be useful around here. I can run errands or whatever you need me to do," said William. He looked at Olivia who wore a look of pure shock as if she had seen a ghost.

"Don't look so surprised," he said. "You know I don't mind helping out."

He wedged a forkful of lasagna and washed it down with ice tea.

Olivia did not say a word.

She continued to stare.

Her jaw fell and her shoulders sank.

After a few seconds, William realized she was not staring at him and she was looking behind him.

Everyone turned to see Dani standing in the living room.

Olivia whispered, "Thank you Jesus."

Leonard walked over to Dani and ushered her to the kitchen table. She crept under the pain of her injuries.

Everyone in the room continued to stare at Dani but was distracted when the doorbell rang again.

Leonard unenthusiastically pulled his chair from under the table and went to answer the door, grumbling with every step.

The others listened as he opened the door and were astounded when he said, "Mr. James Horne, what a surprise."

James Horne. What is James doing here?

She dropped her fork and looked at William.

Tasha began to chew faster and bit her tongue in the process.

Olivia kept her eyes on her plate and pretended not to listen to the conversation at the front door.

"I came by to check on Dani and Olivia."

"We appreciate your dropping by, but we are asking everyone to wait a few more days before visiting. I'll be sure to let them know you stopped by."

"Yes sir. I understand. And please give Gayle my regards."

The ride home was long and awkward. William drove with his eyes on the road and Gayle sat on the passenger side staring out of the window. Neither wanted to initiate what was sure to be an uncomfortable conversation.

Gayle fidgeted in her purse for a while.

"So how long has James Horne been in town?"

Here we go.

"Oh, he lives here now."

"He does?"

William tried desperately to disguise his jealousy. He could not understand why his wife would keep this information to herself.

"When were you going to tell me?"

"I don't know. It just never came up. Anyway, it's no big deal."

William swerved into the other lane but quickly recovered.

"It's no big deal? Your first love is in town; your husband is hundreds of miles away and it's no big deal?"

He approached an intersection and stopped the car at the red light. He looked over at Gayle. She continued to gaze out of the window.

"Why would it be?" said Gayle finally turning to make eye contact.

"Because he was your first love, that's why."

"William, it's not like that."

"Evidently he's comfortable enough to drop in at Olivia's house unannounced."

William paused for a moment. His thoughts began to scramble. He said, "Or was I the one being too familiar? Did I interrupt things with my unannounced visit?"

The light changed from red to green and William was still lost in his thoughts. The driver behind him blew his horn. William placed his foot on the gas petal and continued to drive.

"James is a friend of the family."

"Is he the reason you've been so reluctant to move to New York?"

"Of course not, you are being unreasonable."

When William pulled into the driveway, Gayle quickly grabbed her things. As soon they entered the house, William turned on the lights and threw his keys on the table.

"Gayle, I've done everything you asked me to do. I've got a steady job, I have enough money saved up to move into my own place and I haven't had a drink in months," he said, raising a finger with each example.

Gayle thought about William's claims. It was true. He had done everything she had asked him to do.

"William, you are making great strides ..."

"How close are you and James?"

"What do you mean?"

"Have you kissed him?"

Gayle thought about how close she would come to not being able to answer William's question truthfully. She was tempted to kiss James on more than one occasion.

"It sounds like you are accusing me of something."

"No, I'm not accusing you of anything. Will you please answer my question?"

Gayle reached for William's hand and invited him to sit with her on the couch with her. She took a deep breath and began, "I've seen James a few times; once in the grocery store, in the library a couple of times and he even brought some kids out for the play. We have not kissed and we have not been intimate. Can you say the same thing?"

"What?"

"Can you tell me that you haven't been with any other women while you were in New York?"

Gayle waited nervously for his reply.

"I haven't been with another woman, Gayle. The only woman I want to be with is you."

Gayle's heart softened.

"But the last time you were here, you didn't even… we stayed up all night addressing envelopes."

"I thought that was what you wanted. I ached for you and I ache for you now. I have been trying to take it slow because I did not want to make a wrong move. I didn't want to do the wrong thing."

She believed him.

He believed her.

#####

The next morning Gayle watched her husband as he slept next to her in their bed. William stretched his arms and opened his eyes.

"Good morning," he said with a smile.

"Good morning."

They lay in bed talking for a few minutes. William repositioned himself against the headboard and announced, "I've made a decision."

"You have?"

"I can't stand being away from you any longer. I am determined to find a job here in Louisiana. Even if it means being a janitor or working at a fast food restaurant. I don't want to spend another six months away from you."

Gayle sat up, "You don't have to do that. I have something to tell you. I got an offer from Disney for my screenplay."

"Gayle, that's wonderful. You got an offer from Disney? Wow, I'm so proud of you," he said. He wrapped his arms around her and she melted in his embrace.

"Let's celebrate. I'll take you out to dinner tonight."

"Aren't you going to ask how much they are going to pay me? Don't you want to know how much they offered?"

"Baby I meant it when I said I wanted to support us. That has nothing to do with the offer for your screenplay. I do think that God has blessed you with a great opportunity to help your family. It looks like Olivia and Dani will have some rough days ahead of them."

Gayle looked at her husband with admiration.

"I was thinking the same thing."

Gayle pulled her husband into her and was about to kiss him when the phone rang.

"Hello?"

"Hey Gayle. You still mad at me?" asked Loretta.

Gayle sat up in bed and covered the phone with her hand. "It's Loretta," she whispered.

"Girl, you know we're cool."

"That's great. What have you been up to? Have you gotten any offers?"

William began to plant baby kisses on Gayle's face as she tried to carry on a conversation.

"Lo, let me call you back. William and I were up late last night and we haven't really gotten out of bed yet."

Gayle looked at William and laughed.

"William is there?"

"Yes, he came in last night."

"Well, tell him I said 'hi'," she said sarcastically.

"Y'all stayed up late again last night, huh?"

"We sure did, and there wasn't a query letter or an envelope anywhere in the room."

CHAPTER 66

Olivia

Gayle and William were surprised to see Olivia in the kitchen preparing a meal when they walked in the house.

"Olivia, you shouldn't be on your feet. I will finish cooking. You go sit down," said Gayle.

"This is *my* kitchen and I want to cook for my family. But if you are determined to be in my kitchen, I'll leave the dishes for you to tackle after we eat."

"Where's Leonard? Does he know what you're doing?" asked Gayle.

"Leonard's at work and Tasha's at school. But Dani's in the living room if you want to tell somebody."

William laughed and grabbed the newspaper. He sat at the table and began reading.

Gayle gave Olivia a hug and headed for the living room where she challenged Dani to a game of UNO.

Olivia fried a whole package of bacon, scrambled a carton of eggs and simmered a huge pot of grits. She baked a batch of her homemade biscuits, singing praises as she worked.

"Draw two," yelled Dani.

Olivia smiled and thanked God that Dani was taking a turn in the right direction. Her appetite was returning and she was spending less time sleeping. Olivia prayed that soon Dani would be sleeping in her own bed and going back to school.

"Now you draw four," yelled Gayle.

Dani laughed and it was music to Olivia's ears.

"How much longer before we eat, Olivia? Smelling those biscuits is making my mouth water," said William.

"It shouldn't be too much longer. They need to brown just a little bit more. What's good in the paper?"

"Not much. There's even less in the employment section."

"Employment section? Are you looking for a job?" asked Olivia.

"It would be nice if I could find something here. I'm tired of being away from my wife."

"Thank you Jesus," whispered Olivia.

She pulled the biscuits from the oven.

"What can I fix for my favorite son-in-law?"

William was taken aback. All he could do was smile.

"I believe that was the first time you referred to me as your son-in-law let alone your favorite son-in-law."

"Do you want me to make your plate or not?"

"Yes ma'am. I want a little bit of everything you got."

Olivia piled his plate with a lot of everything.

"Dani, what would you like to eat?"

"Just a little grits please."

"Are you sure that's all you want? Wouldn't you like some eggs?"

"No thank you. I just want a little grits that's all."

Olivia put a little grits and some eggs on Dani's plate.

"What would you like, Gayle?"

"I'll make my own plate as soon as I beat Dani at this game."

"That's not going to happen. Skip, Skip, Reverse, Uno!" said Dani.

Dani threw her last card on the table and the game was over. Dani won.

"I want a rematch when we finish eating."

Gayle reached for Dani and helped her to the table.

William blessed the food and Olivia excused herself, "I'm going to my room to make a couple of phone calls. You guys eat as much as you like."

She walked to her bedroom, sat on the side of her bed, picked up the phone and dialed the number.

"Hello?"

"Hey Joe Ann, its Olivia. How's Aretha?"

"She's doing much better. They're going to let me bring her home next week."

"That's great. Listen I hate to be the bearer of bad news, but there's something I think you should know."

"What's that?"

"Remember when you asked me to check your messages?"

"Uh-huh."

"Well, I fell in love with your answering machine and I asked Leonard to buy one for our house."

"OK."

"Anyway he installed it wrong and instead of recording messages, the machine was recording conversations."

"That's funny."

"I thought so too. Then I overheard a conversation I did not want to hear. Do you know Deacon Samuels from our church?"

"I'm not sure. What about him?"

"I heard him admit to possibly fathering Aretha's child."

Silence.

"Joe Ann are your there?"

"I'm here. Are you sure that's what you heard?"

"I'm sure. I heard that and a few other things. I confronted him about some things he admitted to saying and doing to Dani. Both Dani and I were injured which is why I am calling you with this information. Otherwise I would never tell you something like this over the phone."

Silence.

"Joe Ann?"

"Can I listen to the tape?"

"The police have it now."

"The police? How did they get involved?"

Olivia spent the next few minutes going over the details.

Joe Ann thanked Olivia for the information and said she would be in touch.

Olivia hung up the phone and thought about her friend.

The phone rang and she picked up the receiver.

"Hello?"

"Olivia, how are you?"

It was Samuels.

Olivia pushed record button on the answering machine.

"Samuels, I can't believe you were stupid enough to call here again."

"I thought maybe we could work things out."

The creases in Olivia's forehead grew deeper.

"You really are crazy aren't you?"

"That's what my lawyer says. You know I'm pleading not guilty by reason of insanity."

He let out a sinister laugh.

"What do you want, Samuels?"

"What do I want? I thought that maybe we could come to an agreement. This whole thing was a misunderstanding and I do not see why it has to go any further. It might be better for you, for Dani, for Aretha and even for Gates of Heaven if you dropped the charges."

"What?"

"Let's just call it even. You drop the charges and I will go about my business. Trust me. You'll never hear from me again."

"Not a chance. I've never trusted you and I'm not about to start now."

"How are things at Gates of Heaven?"

"What?"

"How are things at the church? You know I was not to return. Your pastor came to talk to me, and then Deacon Loveless and the Pastor came to talk to me. Maybe you could talk to your husband and get him to put a good word in for me."

"Maybe you should get off this phone before I say something I'll regret."

"How's sweet little Dani doing?"

Olivia called on the name of Jesus and hung up the phone.

CHAPTER 67

Gayle

Olivia was ready to take matters into her own hands again. She called Leonard who came home right away.

Leonard was angry and could not sit still. He paced the floor.

Gayle was in a mild state of shock and disbelief.

It was awkward, but William had to be the voice of reason.

"Thank God you had the presence of mind to press the record button on the answering machine," said William.

"He was recorded last time and he still got out on bail," said Olivia.

"Olivia, I know you're angry, but we need to call the police. This guy is making threats against you, Dani and your church," said William.

"What could he possibly do to the church?" asked Gayle.

"I don't know but the threat was made. This man has no boundaries. We need to call the police," said William.

"We can call the police, but Olivia and Dani are going to need protection from this guy," said Leonard.

"What about school. Dani can't go back to school with Samuels on the loose," said Olivia.

"I agree. Let us hire a tutor. She can finish the rest of the school year at home. And we'll hire someone to watch the house at all times," said Gayle.

"We don't have the kind of money that it will take to hire people to do that," said Olivia.

"I ... we do. We can take care of it," said Gayle. She looked to her husband for consent.

William nodded in agreement.

"You guys don't have that kind of money either. We appreciate the offer, but we have to be realistic," said Leonard still pacing.

"I wanted to wait until everyone was better before I said anything, but I got an offer from Disney for my screenplay."

"You did, that's great," said Olivia.

She walked over to Gayle and gave her a hug. She was proud of Gayle but she could not stop worrying about Dani.

"I'll receive a check this week for whatever remains after the attorney gets done with it, and then under the terms of my contract, I owe them one additional rewrite, if necessary. There may not be a rewrite--I will not know until it makes it through Development. No matter what happens, I will get the first lump sum this week. We do not have to worry about money. We'll hire a tutor and we'll hire around the clock protection."

Olivia and Leonard were speechless.

The phone rang.

Was Samuels crazy enough to call again?

Leonard stared at the phone for a few seconds and then picked up the receiver. Deacon Loveless was on the other end. He called to report that Gates of Heaven Church was on fire.

CHAPTER 68

Olivia

"You need to go," Olivia said to Leonard.

"No I don't."

"Yes, you do. And I'm going with you."

"No, you're not, Olivia."

"I'm going over there, with or without you."

"OK, I'll get my keys."

Leonard drove across town with Olivia praying aloud in the passenger seat.

The closer they got to the church, the thicker the air became. Black smoke towered from miles around. Smokey vapors penetrated the car vents and rose through their nostrils even as they drove with the windows closed.

Leonard slowed down when they entered the neighborhood. Nearby streets were blocked off and traffic was diverted away from the church. He parked along one of the back roads.

"Are you sure you want to do this," ask Leonard.

Olivia nodded.

Leonard got out and walked over to open the door for Olivia. He reached in and helped her out of the car.

"Be careful. Walk slowly and let me know if you start to feel pain."

"I'm fine Leonard," she said with a bit of irritation.

"We are only staying for a little while. We've got to get back to the house."

"I know. I want to get back home and check on Dani."

"She's fine, Olivia. William and Gayle are with her."

"I know. Do you think Samuels had anything to do with this?" she whispered.

"I think he had everything to do with it."

Bits of ashes fell like snow flurries.

Yellow police tape line the area. A group of people gathered watching the rescue workers save what was left of the sanctuary. Reporters stood on one end of the street.

Leonard saw the pastor, Deacon Francis, Deacon and Mother Hamilton and Sister Anderson mobilized a few feet away. He reached for Olivia's hand and meandered his way through the crowd.

They greeted everyone with hugs.

Leonard asked if anyone had seen or heard anything.

"Somebody said they saw a blue Ford Thunderbird parked outside of the church," said Sister Anderson.

Leonard and Olivia looked at each other curiously.

"Why would anybody burn down the House of the Lord? That's just evil," said Mother Hamilton.

"That guy over there in the corner said that he saw Samuels leaving the church minutes before he saw thick black smoke coming from the building," said Deacon Hamilton pointing to a man in a purple jogging suit standing next to the police officer.

The pastor shook his head in disbelief.

Mother Hamilton's eyes began to water.

"Leonard, I think we need to get back home," said a frightened Olivia.

"You're right. Let's get home."

#####

Leonard brought the answering machine into the living room so the uniformed police officers could listen to the taped conversation between Olivia and Samuels.

"This guy thinks he's invincible," said the tall, white police officer with the shiny-bald head. Officer Thomas stood over six feet.

Gayle stared out the kitchen window. Her voice broke when she turned to Officer Thomas and said, "What happens next?"

"He violated the conditions of his release and this cassette proves it, ma'am," he said holding the plastic bag containing the answering machine cassette tape.

"He'll be denied bail this time," added Officer Jones, a short black man with a gold front tooth. "We have probable cause and enough evidence to get a warrant."

The wheels of justice were set into motion.

"Do you mind if I have a look around?" asked Officer Jones.

"Go right ahead," said Leonard putting his arms around his wife.

Officer Jones began to walk around the peripheral of the house looking at everything and nothing in particular.

"It's been a long day. Why don't you get some rest Olivia?" asked Gayle.

"I'm not tired."

"Did you say this man was a deacon at your church?" asked Officer Thomas.

"Yes," said Leonard, "Or he was."

"Did he ever come out and threaten you ma'am?"

"He just asked questions. He asked about the church. He was angry because they asked him not to come back. Then he had the nerve to ask me about Dani."

"And where is Dani now, ma'am?"

"She's resting in my bedroom."

"Have you had any other contact with him?"

"No."

Officer Jones returned to the room, "We got him," he said, replacing his radio to its holster. "Samuels has been taken into custody and will be charged with arson in addition to the other charges."

CHAPTER 69

Olivia

The arraignment was set for ten o'clock the next morning. Leonard and Olivia walked into the courtroom. There was a large platform for the Judge and two desks, one on each side of the judge's platform. A chair surrounded by waist-high walls was adjacent to the Judge's platform. A wooden gate separated the front of the courtroom from the pew-like seats in the back of the courtroom.

Judge Henry Joseph's forehead, nose and mouth were pronounced. He wore a double chin and sagging jowls. He was hard but fair. Spectators filled his courtroom. Some were dressed in everyday street clothes. There were old people, young people, rich people and poor people.

Olivia recognized a few familiar faces. Officers Jones and Thomas sat near the front. The pastor and his wife sat on the back row dressed in their Sunday best. A few deacons and a handful of church members dispersed themselves throughout the seating area.

Samuels' wife was noticeably absent.

Leonard and Olivia sat near the center next to Joe Ann Mills.

"Joe Ann, I wasn't sure if I would see you today," whispered Olivia giving her friend a hug.

"I had to take off work, but I wanted to be here. Thanks for calling me yesterday. I do not know if I remembered to thank you. I was trying to process everything that you were telling me."

"You're welcome. Let's talk after this is over."

"OK."

Everyone watched as the officer removed Samuels' handcuffs. Samuels and his attorney, Mr. Martin Foote stood before the judge.

"Are you Jason Samuels?" asked Judge Joseph.

"Yes."

"Your attorney is Mr. Martin Foote?"

"Yes."

"Were you served with the indictment against you?"

"Yes."

"Have you read it?"

"Yes."

"Have you discussed it with Mr. Foote?"

"Yes."

Judge Joseph read the indictment aloud and asked Samuels if he understood the charges.

"Yes," responded Samuels.

"How do you wish to plead?"

"Not guilty."

There were a few moans and groans from the spectators. The judge banged his gavel and demanded, "Order in the Court."

The judge denied bail.

A date for the pre-trial motion was set.

CHAPTER 70

Gayle

The trial of Jason Samuels began at eight o'clock in the morning on May 4, 1981, in Courtroom twelve of Shreveport's federal district court with Judge Henry Joseph presiding.

Olivia, Leonard, Gayle, William and Joe Ann Mills sat on the second row of the closed courtroom.

Gayle was anxious and felt nauseous. She was on the verge of throwing up.

All twelve jurors listened intently as Attorney Richard Pope talked. A couple of the jurors shook their heads as he explained in detail the abuse endured by the girls at the hands of Deacon Jason Samuels.

"This is making my stomach turn," Gayle whispered to William.

William wrapped his arms around her.

Gayle could feel her breakfast making its way from her stomach and through her throat. She covered her mouth and ran from the courtroom.

William followed.

Gayle reached the ladies' room just in time to expel the contents of her stomach. She freshened up and met William in the hallway.

"Let me take you home."

"No. I'll be fine."

"You don't look so fine."

"I am. I need to stay here with Olivia," she said beginning to grow irritated.

"Leonard is here with Olivia. Let's go home."

"I'm staying here. Let's go back in the courtroom."

William reluctantly followed Gayle into the courtroom where Attorney Pope continued to present his opening statement.

"The mother of victim number one will tell you how she came home to find her daughter unconscious on the floor after a suicide attempt. This mother will also testify that she rushed her daughter to the emergency room where she found out that her teenaged daughter was pregnant."

The tension in the air was as taut as a balloon filled to its capacity and ready to burst.

"Are you all right?" Olivia whispered to Gayle.

"I'm fine. Are you OK?"

Olivia nodded.

Gayle reached for Olivia's hand and listened to Attorney Pope conclude his opening statement.

After two hours of testimony, Judge Joseph dismissed for lunch.

CHAPTER 71

Olivia

Judge Joseph allowed the prerecording of both Aretha's and Dani's testimony. After lunch, jurors watched the recorded sessions with police and psychologists. It took every bit of self-control in Olivia not to jump over the railing and choke the life out of Samuels.

Once again, Gayle grew sick to her stomach and had to leave the courtroom. Joe Ann watched the big screen with tears in her eyes as she listened to the details of Aretha's ordeal. Some of which she heard for the first time.

When it was Olivia's turn to testify she sat forward in the witness chair and nervously picked at her fingernails. Her knees shook. She tried desperately not to look at Samuels for fear of losing control.

The jury members were attentive, some sitting on the edge of their seats.

"Would you state your full name and spell your last name?" asked Attorney Pope, patient and forever proficient.

"Olivia Howard, H-O-W-A-R-D."

"What is your relationship to victim number two?"

"She's my sister."

"The two of you have the same mother and father, but you are more than sisters aren't you?"

"Yes, sir. My husband and I are raising her."

"And why are you raising her?"

"Our parents are deceased."

"How old was Dani when she came to live with you and your husband?"

"She was nine years old."

"How old is she now?"

"She is seventeen."

"How do you know the defendant?"

"He is … or he was a deacon at our church?"

"Mrs. Howard, are you employed?"

"Yes, I am an electrician."

"And did you work on the date in question?"

"Yes, I did."

"And was Dani at home when you arrived?"

"Yes, she was but she left soon after I got home."

"And what happened after she left?"

"I went to my room and took a bath."

"And how long were you in the bath?"

"About twenty minutes."

"What happened after you finished your bath?"

"The phone rang. It was my husband and we talked for a few minutes. Then I listened to the messages on the answering machine."

"And was there anything unusual about the messages?"

"Yes, the machine had recorded phone conversations instead of messages. It was a new machine that my husband had programed the night before."

"Your Honor, the State would offer the cassette tape Exhibit A into evidence."

Attorney Pope held a plastic bag containing the cassette tape in the air like a championship trophy. He removed the cassette and placed it into a recorder.

The courtroom was still as the jury listened to the cassette tape.

One male juror gritted his teeth as he listened to Samuels' threats. A few others shook their heads and one woman's eyes began to water.

When the tape ended, Attorney Pope stood silent, letting the jurors digest Samuels' recorded words.

"And what happened after that?"

"I left a note for my husband, grabbed a skillet and left for the motel."

"And why did you grab a skillet?"

"For protection. I wasn't sure what I'd face when I got to the motel."

"What did you see when you walked into the motel room?"

"I saw Dani lying on the bed and Samuels holding a gun."

Samuels shifted in his seat at the defense table, shook his head and whispered nervously into his lawyer's ear.

The jury listened as Olivia described what took place in the motel room. She testified for nearly an hour and a half, occasionally sipping water from a cup.

Then Attorney Foote cross-examined her for nearly two hours.

At five o'clock, the judge excused the witness and adjourned court for the day.

#####

Across town Samuels sat in a tiny cell measuring ten feet by twelve feet with two bunk beds, a sink and a toilet; all bolted to the floor. Three walls were made of cinder and the fourth consisted of bars. There were no windows and the entire hall stank of urine.

Samuels shared a cell with a man known as Popeye because of his bulging eyes. Popeye was of small statue but he held a reputation for committing crimes such as Breaking and Entering, Theft and Possession of stolen goods. Popeye was no stranger to the justice system.

Samuels sat on the edge of the lower bunk across from Popeye who was asleep on the other lower bunk. The guard opened the cellblock and the two were faced-to-face with another cellmate. The new resident was a large, black man with broad shoulders and an expression that read 'do not disturb'.

The new cellmate sat on the bottom bunk next to Samuels.

"I supposed you want the bottom bunk?" asked Samuels trying not to sound sarcastic.

The new cellmate glared at Samuels who stood to his feet and climbed onto the top bunk, but not before introducing himself.

"My name is Jason Samuels."

"First time Jason?" asked the new cellmate.

"Yeah. How'd you know?"

"First timers don't know when to shut up."

The guard interrupted with dinner.

The new cellmate grabbed one of the three plates. Samuels jumped down from his bunk, grabbed one, and pushed the third one to the side for Popeye.

"What'd you say your name was?" asked Samuels.

"I didn't."

"What'll I call you?"

"Buck."

Samuels rolled his eyes and stuck a piece of stale yeast roll in his mouth.

He washed it down with water.

They dined in silence for a few minutes.

Buck seemed to be in a better mood after filling his belly with rubbery roast beef and Styrofoam mashed potatoes.

"So what you in for?" asked Buck.

"Some young chick practically threw herself at me. She didn't look her age and I wasn't asking. You know what I mean? So what you in for, Buck?" asked Samuels

"Disorderly Conduct, Assault and a couple other things. My ex called me last week and told me my little girl had been hurt." His voice trembled. "There was nothing I could do about it. I could not fix it. She was in a bad way. I wanted to hurt somebody ...anybody. Started drinking and didn't stop until I was punching some dude's lights out in a bar."

Buck stood and slid his empty tray in the corner. He stopped to look at Samuels before lying back on his bed.

"Any more questions?" he asked.

"No Sir, Mister Buck."

CHAPTER 72

Gayle

The following morning Attorney Pope stood before the jury looking more dapper than the day before. He wore a tailor-made three-piece brown suit with a white dress shirt and brown tie. Joe Ann Mills did not consider his looks when he questioned her on the witness stand.

She described finding her daughter unconscious on the floor beside a half-empty bottle of sleeping pills.

"I thought she was playing a joke on me," Joe Ann testified. "We joke around a lot. I told her to stop playing around because I was tired. I had just gotten off work ... She did not move ... I could not believe it. I shook her ... yelled at her ... I did whatever I could to try to wake her. But she just lay there. Then I saw the bottle ... my sleeping pills. Half of the pills were gone."

Judge Joseph handed Joe Ann a tissue.

She wiped her face and blew her nose.

Two of the jury members wiped away tears as well.

"And then what did you do?"

"I picked her up and put her in the car and drove as fast as I could to the hospital."

Joe Ann cried several times on the witness stand during the question and answer routine that ensued. But she openly sobbed when she talked about finding out about the baby.

"The doctor told me that she tried to kill herself and they told me she lost the baby. I didn't even know she was pregnant."

The jury hung on to her every word.

Joe Ann was overcome with emotion and unable to continue.

Judge Joseph called for a recess.

During his closing, Attorney Pope told the jurors that Samuels had cooked up a pot of insanity gumbo and he was offering it with all the fixings.

"But you don't have to accept it. If you don't trust the ingredients in the gumbo, don't trust the cook, you don't have to swallow the gumbo."

Attorney Foote concluded his closing statements by reminding jurors that a verdict of not guilty by reason of insanity would not set Samuels free. Judge Joseph would decide when, if ever, Samuels would be released.

Judge Joseph read the jury instructions and at three forty-five, the jury began deliberations.

#####

Mrs. Faye's Soul Food restaurant was as old as the city of Shreveport. The ten tables were the original ones brought in just before the place opened.

Seating was never a problem because Mrs. Faye's was located in the heart of downtown and the regulars were lawyers, paralegals and secretaries who picked up a to-go plate and took it back to their busy offices.

Attorney Pope suggested Mrs. Faye's place for a late lunch while they waited for the jury to deliberate.

"Just sit anywhere," said the server behind the cash register. "I'll be with you in a moment."

Leonard looked around the room and spotted two empty tables near the back of the room.

"Is it alright if we push two tables together?" he asked.

"Sure, hon. Pick the two that you want and I'll be right with you."

The men pushed the two tables together and everyone took a seat.

"How many y'all got?" asked the server.

"There'll be six of us," said William.

"OK. You want to order your drinks now or wait for the rest of the party?"

The server counted out six napkins, and six sets of plastic silverware.

Attorney Pope walked in the door and they decided to order drinks.

"Y'all can go ahead and help yourselves when you're ready. The plates are at the end of the buffet."

When everyone had his or her drinks and a plate of food, Leonard said grace.

"I'm sorry I kept y'all waiting," said Joe Ann, joining the others at the table. I was trying to get a hold of Buck."

"Buck? How is Buck? I didn't know y'all were still in touch with each other," asked Olivia.

"He's doing alright. I told him everything that happened. He kept asking questions about Samuels. He wanted to know his full name, who his family was and stuff like that."

She took a deep breath and a sip of tea.

"Buck blames himself. Said if he was around more often, this would not have happened. I don't think I've ever heard him this mad."

"I'm surprised he wasn't in court," said Gayle.

"He said he was coming. It is probably a good thing that he did not make it because he said he was going to blow Samuels' head off."

Everyone looked at Pope.

"You didn't hear that," said William.

Pope smiled and took a bite of his fried pork chop.

"When I didn't see him in court," Joe Ann continued, "I tried to call his mama from the pay phone during recess. She had not heard from him since last night. She said he was probably out drinking. Thank God he's not my problem anymore."

"What ever happened to that woman ..." asked Olivia.

"That hussy he left me for?"

"Yeah, that one."

"They broke up a long time ago. He did the same thing to her that he did to me. Now he's talking about how much he loves Aretha and how he wants to make up for not being there for her."

A long silence followed as everyone thought about what to say next.

"How do you think the jury will vote?" William asked Pope.

"In my opinion, a verdict other than guilty is a long shot. Crucial elements needed for insanity is missing," said Pope.

"I mean, haven't we all had a rough childhood in one way or the other?" said Gayle.

Samuels returned to his jail cell where he found Buck resting on one of the bottom bunks and Popeye resting on the other. Samuels climbed on one of the top bunks and sat with his feet dangling off the side.

Buck stood up, pointed at the bed where Samuels sat and said, "I think I want that bunk now?" Samuels rolled his eyes and jumped down.

Without a word, Buck kicked his feet from under him causing him to fall to the floor. Samuels curled himself into a defensive position with his knees pulled in toward his chin.

Buck commenced with a swift kick to Samuels' temple.

Samuels' head fell back against brick wall.

Samuels uttered a series of profanities.

"I talked to my ex this morning. She gave me the name of the bastard that hurt my little girl," said Buck administering another swift kick to the rib.

The beating continued.

"Don't - nobody - mess - with - me - or - mine - and - get - get - away - with - it!" said Buck, grunting a word with every blow.

Samuels shrieked in pain.

"Get up!"

Samuels stood despite the excruciating pain and Buck delivered a right cross to Samuels left jaw.

Popeye signaled that the guard was coming.

Buck backed away leaving Samuels on the floor against the wall, his body throbbing from the crown of his head to the soles of his feet.

The guard opened the door and cautiously scrutinized the surroundings.

"What's going on here?" he asked.

Popeye looked away.

Buck sneered.

No one answered.

"If y'all don't know, then I don't know," replied the guard.

"Samuels, they want you back in court."

Samuels grimaced, closed his eyes and limped away clutching his stomach.

CHAPTER 73

Olivia

Leonard, Olivia, William, Gayle, Joe Ann and Attorney Pope joined hands and formed a circle in the hallway before entering the courtroom. Leonard asked God to prepare their hearts to receive whatever lay ahead.

Samuels entered the courtroom with a limp, a swollen lip and sore ribs.

"Wonder what happened to him?" whispered Leonard.

Joe Ann smiled.

The jury entered and Attorney Pope felt a sense of relief when one of the jurors made eye contact with him.

Everyone stood as Judge Joseph entered.

"Madam Foreman, have you reached a verdict?"

"Yes, we have?"

The foreman handed the verdict to the clerk, who handed it to Judge Joseph. Judge Joseph read the paper and returned it to the clerk who returned it to the Jury Foreman.

It took the jury two-and-a-half hours to reject the insanity plea and return a verdict of guilty on all charges.

CHAPTER 74

Dani

Four Months Later

Dani peered through her bedroom window into the neighborhood where she spent most of her childhood. It was a beautiful September day clothed in sunshine, and a cool gentle breeze occupied the air. It was time for the college freshman to check into the dorms at Grambling and Gayle was helping her pack for the move.

"You're going off to college, girl."

She folded another t-shirt and handed it to Dani.

"I know. I am just glad I made it through Chemistry class. I wasn't sure I'd make it."

"I'm tired. I going to take a short break," said Gayle. She pushed some clothes to the side sat on Dani's bed. Her unexpected pregnancy brought joy to the entire family. The nausea subsided after the first trimester but now she could not eat enough.

"I can't believe you're having a baby," said Dani.

"Me neither. I have a human being growing inside of me."

Monday mornings were usually chockfull of preparations for work and school but this Monday morning took a different course. Leonard planned to go into work late, Olivia gave Tasha permission to go to school late and Olivia was not going to work at all. Even William and Gayle rearranged their schedules and flew in from New York for the occasion.

"If you forget something, you can always get it when you come home for the weekend," said Gayle.

She adjusted her back against the headboard.

"That's right. I can come home on the weekends, can't I?"

"You're only ninety minutes up the road."

Dani relaxed a bit and folded another t-shirt.

Gayle rubbed her tiny baby bump.

"The baby's moving. You want to feel it?"

Dani reached for her sister's belly. Gayle guided Dani's hand to a spot just below her ribcage.

"Do you want a boy or a girl?"

"The last time I was asked that question, God gave me a little sister," said Gayle referring to a conversation she had with their mother when she was pregnant with Dani. "But this time, I want to be surprised."

Dani offered a weak smile. Gayle placed her hand on top of Dani's hand.

She hesitated before speaking again.

"If your life were a script, how would you write the next chapter?"

"I would eliminate Samuels."

"That's been done. He is in prison and will be there for a long time. What else would you write?"

"I would write that I finished college and …"

The phone rang.

"Dani, telephone," yelled Tasha from another room in the house.

Dani walked over to the nightstand and picked up the phone.

"I got it," she yelled to Tasha.

"Hello?"

"Hey girl. It's me, Aretha."

"Hey Aretha."

"Are you packed and ready to go?"

"Almost. Gayle's helping me."

"Gayle's back?"

"Yes. She and William flew in last night."

"Does she look pregnant?"

"She's showing a little bit, but not much. I felt the baby move a few minutes ago."

"Dani?"

"Yeah?"

"I'm really sorry ..."

"Don't say anymore. We have forgiven each other, right?"

"Right."

"Then we're cool, right?"

"Right."

"And we are going to write to each other once a week."

"Right."

They sat silently on the phone for a few seconds.

"Well, Daddy's at the door. I just wanted to wish you well before you left," said Aretha.

"Thanks. Tell Mr. Buck I said hello. I'll write you soon."

"Bye."

Dani hung up the phone and sat next to Gayle on the bed.

"How's Aretha?"

"She fine. Her daddy's taking her to school."

"I'm so glad that something good came out of this. Aretha and her dad have a relationship now."

"Yeah. She is really happy about that. He got a job working at Libby Glass in Shreveport and he promised to stay in town at least until she graduates. He comes over for breakfast every morning before school and she spends the weekends at his house."

"Did he ever admit to beating up Samuels?"

"No, but we all know that he did it."

There was a knock at the door and Olivia entered the room.

"It's almost time to go," she said.

"Olivia, feel my stomach. The baby is moving," said Gayle.

Olivia walked over and put her hand on Gayle's stomach.

She smiled.

"I think he's going to be a kicker for the Dallas Cowboys."

Gayle laughed.

"Dani and I were talking about the next chapter in her life."

Dani sat on the bed.

"I'm so sorry for everything, Olivia."

"Listen, Dani. You just focus on your future. Samuels was the adult and he should have known better. I just wish ..."

A hush fell over the room.

Tears fell from every eye.

Gayle tried to change the mood.

"Olivia, what do you want the baby to call you? Auntie or Granny? Or maybe Auntie Granny?

Somehow, the name seemed appropriate because after all they were more than sisters.

About the Author

W. Mason Dunn is the sixth of six children born to Reverend and Mrs. Walter Mason Senior. The native Louisianan has lived in Texas, California, Virginia, North Carolina and most recently Florida.

After earning her master's degree in Public Administration from The University of Oklahoma, W. Mason Dunn worked in various capacities of higher education.

She and her husband live in Tallahassee, Florida and have two grown children.

In her spare time, she enjoys reading, writing and solving complex crossword puzzles.